THE PROGRAM

A NOVELLA

CARY REED

URGESTA AS

CONTENTS

THE PROGRAM

A NOVELLA

CARY REED

URGESTA AS

THE PITCH

The boy sat on the hospital bed with his back to the door, staring at—or through—the window. From the hall, the man couldn't tell which. In the next room, a television replayed the news of John Lennon's murder. Here, there was only silence. The boy's roommate lay in a near-coma. The boy might as well have been, too.

The man hung his coat on the hook and stepped inside. The boy didn't turn. Legs dangling, shoulders slumped, left arm in a sling, right arm limp.

Outside, a snowplow's yellow light swept the across darkness. Its blade scraped through ice, scattering salt. Across the street, the park lay buried—merry-go-round, see-saw, forgotten toys—under a clean white shroud.

The boy looked at him then. Annoyance, not curiosity. The man dropped the file on the table.

"May I?" the man asked, motioning to the hard plastic chair. He didn't wait for permission. The legs scraped against the linoleum as he pulled it into the boy's line of sight and sat.

"You see that file?" He tipped his chin toward the table. "It tells me almost everything about you—probably more than you'd like me to know."

The boy finally spoke. "What's in it?"

"Metrics," the man said. "Height, weight, reflexes... intelligence. Every number, every note, from some of the smartest men in this city. They've poked, prodded, and tested you, and they've written it all down."

"Why?"

"To see if you're a candidate."

"For what?"

"You're a ward of the state," the man said. "Know what that means?" The boy shook his head. "It means you're headed into 'The System.' Foster parents, if they can find any. Otherwise, a group home. That's just the new word for an orphanage. People think changing the label changes the thing. It doesn't." He let that hang for a moment. "Is that where you want to end up?"

He leaned forward, hands clasped loosely between his knees, eyes locked on the boy. "What if there was another path? A program built for kids like you. Food, shelter, a first-rate education. The chance to become something more than just a name in a file. But you'd have to learn what we teach you. Not just learn—master it. You know what that means?"

"Doing something until you get it right," the boy said.

A slow smile spread across the man's face. "No. It means doing it until you can't get it wrong."

The boy said nothing. His eyes stayed fixed on the space between them, as if something there held him.

"What if I can't?" he asked at last.

"You can," the man said, tapping the file. "That's what this tells me. What it can't tell me is if you will. That's yours to decide."

He sat back, certain the hook was set. But the boy didn't bite. If anything, his shoulders sank lower.

"What do you want?" the man asked.

The boy raised his head. Dark eyes, steady. "To go home. To be normal. Like everyone."

It hit the man in a place he didn't like to think about. Natural. Pathetic. The same, somehow.

"I... don't think that's in the cards," he said, clearing his throat as he stood. "Sorry, kid."

He lifted the file, slid a business card into its place. "If you want something different... maybe even better—call that number."

Then he left him as he'd found him—alone, staring out the window.

Snow was falling again by the time the man reached the garage. He slowed as he passed the park, glancing up at the hospital wing. The windows were dark. If the boy was still there, he was lost in the shadows. The man turned away. Another building waited. Another face in another window.

THE GIRL WITH HEARTS IN HER WINDOW

Part 1: W650

Ignoring the cramps was my first mistake.

They'd started that morning, faint pulses I tried to pretend weren't there. By the time I was sparring with Aaliyah in the Krav Maga pit, they felt like a knife twisting in my gut. She grabbed my shoulder, planted her knee in my stomach, and I doubled over, biting back a groan. I was thirteen, clutching a red pad, trying to block her hits while ignoring the dull ache spreading through my body.

No girl's first period is exactly a celebration of blossoming womanhood—I'd heard enough horror stories to know that. And while mine wasn't as bad as that scene from Carrie, it still fucking sucked.

Our instructors didn't care. At *The Fort*, pain wasn't an excuse. Aaliyah and I were just "recruits," sweating through Phase 2 of *The Program*, learning to block, strike, and dodge like our lives depended on it. And maybe one day they would. Compared to the luxury of Phase 1—*The Campus*, where we'd spent the last few years learning languages and sitting through dehumanizing health films from the '70s—The Fort was a brutal place. Here, humidity was the air you breathed, sweat was your second skin, and even the porta-potties at the training grounds seemed designed to break us.

We were blank slates, stripped of even our names. I was still W650, or "Whiskey Six-Five-Zero," though Aaliyah had already chosen a real name for herself, after her late sister. I just wasn't sure what I wanted to be called yet—or even who I wanted to be.

For most of us, The Program was the only choice: college, paid in full, if we stuck it out. A shot at something stable. It wasn't a family, not exactly, but it was a kind of security. And after a year here, I already knew what the alternative looked like—*The System*, they called it, where kids like me usually ended up. The Program didn't replace parents, but it sure beat the uncertainty waiting outside its walls.

Here, survival was everything. By the end of the first year at The Fort, almost half of us girls were gone. Those of us who were left enjoyed some unexpected perks—hot water in the showers, no line for the sinks. But as our numbers thinned, the expectations only grew heavier, the training more relentless. I couldn't tell if I was getting stronger or just harder, or if that was the same thing.

And then, of course, there was the whole mess of growing up. Sexuality, identity—all of it tangled up in a place that didn't have room for either. The only time we saw the boys was once a year at the holidays. By the time we were reunited with them for good, they'd changed—deeper voices, patchy facial hair, body odor, and odd senses of humor.

But back to my period...

Aaliyah, convinced she'd just destroyed my internal organs, looked on the verge of tears. She gripped my hand, swearing she'd quit The Program if I got kicked out because of her. Sweet of her, but unnecessary.

If The Program had taught me one thing to that point, it was how to grit my teeth and keep going.

"Hold up!" a cadre called out as she approached, looking at my crotch. "Whiskey Six-Five-Zero, take your gear and go to the medics! Hustle!"

The medics' quarters smelled like antiseptic and stale cigarette smoke. The female soldiers who worked there weren't much older than us, though at the time, they seemed ancient. One of them—a gruff woman named O'Connor with a thick Boston accent—took one look at me and grimaced.

"Great," she muttered, clearly disappointed. "We usually get wicked gnarly broken bones and shit. I get the chick with her first period."

She yanked open a drawer and held up two packages: one pink and bulky, the other purple and compact. "Pick your poison."

I stared at them, mystified. "How do they... work?"

O'Connor sighed. "One goes on. The other goes in."

"Can't you just give me something to make it stop?" I asked, feeling my face flush as the other medics chuckled.

"Nope, honey," one of them—Vell—said. "But hey, welcome to womanhood." She raised her eyebrows at me. "Don't nobody be teachin' you girls about this stuff?"

"We saw a video," Aaliyah offered.

O'Connor rolled her eyes. "Well, kid, it only gets worse."

I blinked, horrified. "Worse?"

"Not the bleeding. I mean being a woman." She waved us outside.

At the smoking area, she lit up and gestured at the buildings around us. "None of this is the real world. Out there? They want you sexy, but not too sexy. Smart, but not smarter than them."

"Who's them?" I asked.

"Men," Vell said simply. "Whole world's run by 'em. And they like women a certain way."

Fleck, the third medic, chimed in: "Be pretty, but not too pretty. Thin, but not skinny. Tough, but not pushy. And if you like a guy? Don't tell him. Just laugh at his jokes and hope he asks you out."

By the time they were done, my head was spinning from all the contradictions. The Fort's rules were brutal, but at least they were clear. Out there, womanhood sounded like a maze with no exit.

When we got back to Krav Maga, I was almost relieved.

As usual, they rotated sparring partners so nobody got too comfortable. My luck ran out when I got paired with Joelle—Jo—the closest thing The Program had to a machine. We thought she was the ideal recruit: powerful, unyielding, terrifying. On Sundays, while most of us rested or zoned out in front of the TV on our only day off, Jo lifted weights. She felt less like a girl my age and more like a force of nature.

A cadre bellowed "Grab a handful of sand!" through a megaphone. We were in the pit—sand and wood chips soaking up every drop of sweat, spit, and blood. "Rub it in your opponent's hair!"

Jo didn't hesitate. She scooped a fistful and dumped it onto my head. My hair was pulled back tight, but she had a gift for making sure it got everywhere. My attempt to return the favor ended in a pitiful sprinkle over her shoulder. She looked more insulted than threatened.

We squared off, her gaze steady, deadly.

She murmered, "Saw you earlier. That time of the month?" She even managed a half-sneer. Impressive, in its way.

"Fight!" the instructor yelled.

I threw a jab; she slipped it and drove a strike into my gut that folded me in half.

"Get up, Whiskey Six-Five-Zero!" a cadre screamed in my face. "Go at her! Be aggressive!"

I forced myself up, aimed a low kick at her knee. She sidestepped and answered with a brutal knee to my midsection—right where Aaliyah had nailed me earlier. My arms shook as I tried to block, but Jo pressed the attack. She saw the hesitation, took her opening, and smashed her forearm into the side of my head.

Down I went, like a sack of—let's go with "potatoes." I've cussed enough for one day.

***

The next morning, sporting a fresh welt from yesterday's sparring, I laced up my shoes for another run. Some days it was distance, other days sprints. I preferred the long runs—not because I enjoyed running, but because they took us past the barracks.

Our "barracks" weren't the rows of bunk beds and lockers you might picture. They were more like cramped apartments, four girls to a room with two windows. When we ran, we passed the buildings where the soldiers lived. From the outside, they looked the same as ours—except for one window on the third floor, which stood out with pink curtains and heart-shaped stickers.

On those runs, when my legs burned and my lungs felt ready to burst, my thoughts drifted to that window. I'd fix my gaze on those heart stickers as we ran past, imagining what the room looked like inside. I pictured a plant with big, glossy leaves, a purple beanbag chair in the corner, and walls of warm, exposed brick—things that had no place in The Fort.

In that room, I wasn't W650. I had a real name, one I'd chosen myself, and a life that felt like mine. Outside the window, there was no harsh training ground, just a quiet street in a small town, like the ones I'd seen on TV. Boutique shops and cozy cafes, a tree reaching its branches toward the glass....

I'd imagine the person who lived there: someone with a job she actually liked—maybe an actress, or a journalist, or even a doctor. Her apartment would be filled with books, a small but good-quality stereo, and a closet packed with thrift-store treasures. She'd have a kind boyfriend who made her laugh, and a cat—definitely a cat, orange and white, with a perfect pink nose. On chilly mornings, she'd walk to the café on the corner where the barista knew her order, and sometimes slipped her a free muffin with a wink.

It was like evidence of life beyond The Program—something that might seem obvious to everyone on the outside looking in, but not to us. Maybe I'd get there. I just wasn't sure who I would be if and when I did.

After morning PT, we hit the showers. I lingered, examining the fresh bruises that had bloomed on my arms and legs like battle scars.

"You've got to be more aggressive," a voice echoed off the tiles. It was Jo. Stripped down, she looked even more imposing. I hadn't realized the human stomach had that many muscles.

"What?"

"In the pit," she said, lathering up. "You've gotta ramp it up. Everywhere, really. That's what they're looking for."

"I know," I said, a little defensively. "I'm just... not sure it's what I want."

She snorted. "Newsflash!" Yeah, we still said that back then. "Nobody cares what you want. They say learn Russian, we learn Russian. They say run, we run." She shrugged. "I come from the system. Going back's not an option. Here, I get fed, I have clothes, and I don't have to worry about some creepy foster dad sneaking into my room at night. I'll take it."

I let her words sink in. Jo's reality was different from mine. For her, this place was better than anything she could imagine was waiting outside, and she'd adapted to it without looking back. But for me, that quiet room with the purple beanbag and the cat was a lifeline that still called to me.

"I don't think we're supposed to wear those in the shower," Jo said, nodding at my crotch.

I looked down, horrified to realize I was still clutching a swollen, soggy pad between my thighs. "I think you're right," I told her.

Mercifully, that was the last time I had to spar with Jo for a while. We moved on to reconnaissance and infiltration, learning how to spot and evade security measures of all kinds. And if evasion didn't work? We learned how to defeat those measures—usually by blowing them up.

Our instructors in this phase of training were all military, and their solutions to problems were straightforward: apply force in the right place, at the right time, to achieve maximum effect. One of their favorite sayings was, "If brute force doesn't work, you're not using enough." They might've meant it as a joke, but only halfway.

***

Most Sundays, I lost myself playing soccer, letting the rhythm of the game and the ache in my legs drown out everything else. But that week, I dragged Aaliyah to the gym instead. I'd been there before, but never on a Sunday. If I was supposed to be more like Jo, this seemed like a good place to start.

The gym was alive with sharp cries, grunts, and the heavy thud of bodies hitting mats.

"Again!" a man's voice barked, echoing off the walls.

In the weight room, Jo and some of the others were lifting under a cadre's watchful eye, their faces set in hard lines. But what caught my attention was a small group gathered in an adjacent room, where two soldiers were squaring off in the center of a mat.

"Let's go lift," Aaliyah muttered, tugging my arm. "I have enough bruises."

"Wait," I whispered, transfixed by the fight.

One of the soldiers was a towering, beefy guy who looked like he belonged on a football field. The other was shorter, lean, almost unassuming—at least until he moved.

The big guy lunged, his fist hurtling toward his opponent like a battering ram. My heart clenched. I'd been on the receiving end of hits like that in Krav Maga—hits that relied on pure, punishing strength. But the smaller soldier didn't flinch. He shifted his weight, sidestepped, and caught the larger man's wrist with a fluid twist of his arm. His other hand slid to the back of the attacker's elbow. With a smooth pivot, he redirected the larger soldier's momentum, sending him crashing to the mat. It was graceful. Elegant, even.

"Ho-ly shit," Aaliyah said—perhaps a bit too loudly.

Heads turned. Even the soldier on the mat looked our way, a bemused expression on his face.

"Sorry," I mumbled, pulling Aaliyah back.

"Hold up," the instructor called, walking over with a smile. He was tall and lean, with a calm, easy energy that felt out of place at The Fort. "Names?"

"Whiskey Seven-Nine-Six," Aaliyah said.

"Whiskey Six-Five-Zero," I replied.

"I'm Sergeant Creek," he said. "You can call me Eric. Or *Sensei*, here."

"Sensei?" The word felt strange in my mouth, almost reverent. This wasn't like our usual cadre, who barked orders and treated us like machines. "What is this?" I asked, glancing back at the lean soldier, who was now helping his opponent to his feet.

"Aikido," Creek answered.

It wasn't a word I'd ever heard around here. Everything else we learned was blunt, brutal, designed to break things—or people. But this was something different, something that seemed to flow rather than clash.

"Can we... can we learn that?" I asked, feeling a flutter of excitement.

The agile soldier chuckled, glancing at Creek, who raised an eyebrow and smiled. "With time," he said. "If you're willing to put in the effort. Come on, join us."

I looked at Aaliyah, unsure if she'd go for it. But her eyes were as wide as mine, and the look on her face told me everything I needed to know. She was hooked. So was I.

As I stepped onto the mat for the first time, I felt an unexpected thrill, a sense that maybe—just maybe—there were other ways to survive this place. I met Creek's eyes, and he nodded, as if he understood.

"Let's get started," he said.

***

Each Sunday, like clockwork, Aaliyah and I returned to Eric's dojo. Any stolen moments in between were dedicated to practice—refining our turns, perfecting our holds, practicing each movement until it felt like muscle memory. Aikido became a passion unlike anything else in my life, a quiet obsession that kept pulling me back to the mat.

The more I practiced, the more I realized Aikido was as much a mental exercise as a physical one. It felt like a dialogue with my opponent, a silent conversation built on instinct and intention. Instead of meeting force with force, I was learning to shift the conversation, to let my opponent's energy guide my response. The Program had taught me to survive through sheer strength and courage; Aikido was teaching me the art of flow.

At first, I struggled. Techniques like *irimi-nage*—where you step into an attack to blend with it—felt counterintuitive, almost impossible. My instinct screamed at me to resist, to brace myself, to strike back. But Eric's mantra was always the same: *yield to win* he'd say in that calm, steady voice, like it was the simplest thing in the world. *Yield to win.*

It went against every fiber of my being. Yielding felt like giving up. But over time, as I kept practicing, something shifted. I began to understand that power didn't always have to be about domination. Sometimes, it was about redirection—about letting things flow around you rather than forcing your way through. With every turn, every redirection, I started to feel a different kind of strength—one that didn't rely on aggression but on control, harmony, and balance.

This wasn't just a change in how I fought; it was a shift in how I approached everything. Each time I successfully redirected an attack, deflected a strike, or felt the give-and-take of a technique coming together, it reinforced something deeper—a kind of self-belief I hadn't felt before. Aikido made me feel powerful in a way The Program never had. And it made me think there was more than one way to be strong.

But that realization came with its own dangers. The Program wanted us confident, yes, but a certain kind of confident—the kind that followed orders, met aggression with aggression, and didn't question the rules. If I went too far down this road, I could be seen as weak, or worse—unfit. I'd seen others fail out for less.

Every Sunday, I was reminded that I was walking a fine line. I was learning things The Program hadn't intended me to learn, and I knew that if I slipped—if I couldn't keep up with both worlds—I'd risk being rejected entirely.

But it felt worth the risk.

Part 2: The Turn

After a month of relentless training, the time had come for us to face a series of "field problems" designed to test our reconnaissance and infiltration skills. We were split into teams of ten, rotating leadership roles for each of the ten missions. Every morning, we'd get our briefing with the day's objective—surveillance, targeted infiltration, or extraction. Every night, we'd debrief, dissecting each team's choices in brutal detail, noting every mistake and missed opportunity.

The next day, the missions would be totally different—all of them, that is, but one. That first night, W938 was the designated leader for her team. "The target is a high-value individual residing in this compound," she said, clicking to a slide that showed a two-story house, heavily fortified, fenced in on all sides. The familiar landscape of The Fort loomed in the background, but the building itself looked like a fortress. She pointed to various points on the slide. "Two guards inside, two on the roof, one at the gate, and four on standby in the guard shack here."

Major Hicks, an Army officer who rarely showed up for these briefings, took over. She placed a steady hand on W938's shoulder, as if trying to soften the blow. "This problem is hard," she admitted, her voice low but firm. "Team Three-Zero had a solid plan—a feint to draw out the Quick Reaction Force, followed by a counterattack. They breached successfully... but they couldn't account for what awaited them inside." She paused, letting that sink in. "They were nearly annihilated."A hush fell over the room. Hicks' gaze traveled over each of us, her eyes intense, as if she were sizing us up—measuring who would rise to this challenge and who would fold."

That's why we're asking for volunteers to lead this mission instead of assigning them," she said. "And we're offering a reward for anyone who completes this mission successfully."

The slide changed, and the screen filled with the image of our prize. A collective gasp rippled through the room, and suddenly, the impossible mission didn't seem quite so impossible.I wasn't a Joelle. She was the star of The Program, the one everyone expected to lead and win. I was somewhere in the middle of the pack—solid, but not exceptional. But in that moment, something clicked into place. I felt a strange, fierce determination bubble up, a conviction sharper and stronger than anything I'd felt before. And I knew...

I was going to get those fucking Snickers bars.

For days, the HVP mission chewed through every team that faced it. We tried watching for patterns in their failures, but the briefings only gave us glimpses, and the fortress never cracked. I carried that weight with me into Sunday.

Aaliyah and I were early to the dojo. The place smelled faintly of sweat and pine cleaner. Eric was sweeping the mats. Tom, the big guy we'd seen get dumped the first time we came here, was leaning against the wall.

"You look like you're carrying the world on your back," he said. "Rough week?"

I stepped onto the mat, shrugging. "I don't know. Just... not sure this Aikido stuff really works."

Eric set the broom aside and gave me a look halfway between curious and amused. "Doesn't work, huh? Tom—come here."

They squared off. Tom lunged with a straight punch. Eric didn't block—he turned. My eyes followed the smooth pivot of his hips, his hand sliding to Tom's wrist, and in a blink, the big guy was on the mat, staring up at the ceiling.

"That's *tenkan*," Eric said. "You don't stop the strike. You let it keep going... and lead it where you want." He offered Tom a hand up. "If I'd blocked, I'd be fighting his strength with mine. This way, his own momentum did the work."

Aaliyah and I took turns trying it. My hands were clumsy, my timing off. Eric nudged my hip until the movement felt almost weightless.

"Better," he said. "You're not just defending—you're steering."

I frowned. "Feels... opposite of The Program."

He crouched so we were eye level. "One teaches you to dominate. The other teaches you to flow. Both take strength. The trick is knowing when to use which."

I hesitated. "And if flowing doesn't work? If I adapt and just end up booted out?"

He held my gaze, his voice quieter now. "Adaptation isn't weakness. It's survival. The strongest people know how to bend without breaking. In the end, you decide what strength means to you."

***

We all waited for Joelle's turn with bated breath. If anyone could break the losing streak, it was her—The Program's golden girl, the embodiment of everything they drilled into us: strength, discipline, aggression... But when Jo walked into the debrief room that night, the usual swagger was gone. Her confidence had hardened into something brittle. She'd tried a large-scale diversion—an explosion along the perimeter meant to draw the guards out. Instead, it triggered a full lockdown, trapping her team. They scrambled for an alternate route, tried the sewers, but ran out of time before reaching the target.

Seeing Jo rattled sent a chill through the room. If she couldn't do it, what chance did the rest of us have?

The next morning, it was my team's turn. No one volunteered to lead. Failing the "impossible" mission could tank your standing, and nobody wanted that stain on their record. But as I scanned the room and saw everyone avoiding my eyes, something in me hardened. My hand was already halfway up before I realized what I was doing.

I hesitated, just for a heartbeat, then kept it raised. The cadre marked my name with a brief nod, and panic surged in my chest. Smart move or dumb, it was too late now.

We began reconnaissance mid-morning from an abandoned house near the compound. Aaliyah and I hunkered down with binoculars, scanning guard rotations while the rest of the team searched from other vantage points, hunting for anything earlier teams had missed.

"How about cutting the power down the road, then hitting from multiple angles?" Aaliyah murmured.

"Maybe," I said, but my gut wasn't buying it. We'd seen how fast the compound locked down at the first sign of trouble. We needed something quieter.

"Bribe a guard?" she joked.

I snorted. "They don't even leave the compound." We sighed in unison, tossing ideas back and forth while radio updates trickled in.

Around noon, an Army truck rumbled up the road, coughing black smoke with every shift. It looked like the standard supply trucks we saw at The Fort."

That's got to be the truck one team tried sneaking in with," Aaliyah whispered.

"Must be," I said, watching the guards search it before waving it through.

"Huh... I guess they eat the same slop we do," she added, glancing at Sergeant Price, our cadre for the day. Price didn't react.

"What makes you say that?" I asked.

"I saw that same truck near the mess hall this morning—tear in the canvas, patched with green hundred-mile-an-hour tape."

I raised my binoculars. She was right. The driver and another soldier were unloading marmites—big metal containers for hot or cold food. Guards handed over empty ones in exchange for full ones. Quick, no fuss.

"Sure it's the same truck?" I asked.

"Absolutely."

I lowered my binoculars and looked at her. "All the others met force with force. What if we steer their force our way instead?"

Aaliyah's grin was small but knowing. She didn't know my plan yet, but she knew where it was coming from.

I glanced at Sgt. Price. Whatever was in my face made her uneasy; she raised an eyebrow, waiting.

"Sergeant, I think I have an idea," I said.

"Let's hear it."

I laid it out—risky, but simple. If we could get into that truck, or even slip something inside, it could be our ticket in. Price and Aaliyah both looked skeptical, but I kept going until the whole plan was on the table.

Price studied me in silence, her expression unreadable. My pulse pounded. After weeks of failure, this felt like our one chance to try something different.

Finally, she nodded. "You can proceed. But I want constant updates. If anything goes wrong, we pull back immediately. Understood?"

"Yes, Sergeant."

I looked at Aaliyah, who looked back at me with wide eyes. "Come on," I said. "Let's go see the medics."

Part 3: Balance

Under the cloak of darkness, I crouched low with my team, eyes fixed on the winding road through the woods. Every rustle of leaves, every faint hum of an engine tightened the knot in my stomach. Beside me, Aaliyah and the two tallest girls gripped their weapons, knuckles white.

"Positions," I whispered into my radio, nodding to each girl in turn. We'd rehearsed this moment endlessly, but reality made everything sharper, heavier. This wasn't a drill. If we failed, it wasn't just the mission on the line—it was my chance to prove my way could work.

Aaliyah drew a steadying breath. "You ready for this?"

"Hell, yeah," I whispered back, aiming for confidence, though my voice trembled. We almost laughed—nervous, brittle—but an approaching engine froze the sound in our throats.

Minutes stretched like hours until the low, steady rumble of the ambulance cut through the quiet.

"Let's go," I said, my pulse pounding. We stepped into the road and set up our makeshift checkpoint—two white-and-orange reflective barriers we'd dragged from storage. In the stillness, they looked almost official. The ambulance rounded the bend, headlights glaring like the eyes of a wary animal.

It slowed to a stop, idling a few feet away. The others closed in from the sides, weapons trained on the driver and passenger. Sergeant Price stepped forward to greet them, her voice calm, almost warm. She handled them with disarming ease, coaxing them out of the vehicle while keeping the tension hidden beneath a thin layer of authority.

Minutes later, we were climbing in ourselves. Price drove—she was the only one who could. In the back, we adjusted the medics' uniforms, hiding weapons under baggy scrubs. I checked my watch. Just over an hour before the food took effect. I'd worried the spiked meals might be too slow—or fail entirely—but O'Connor had been confident.

"Don't worry," she'd said, watching us mix the powder with casual disinterest. "It'll work wicked fast."

She was right.

When we reached the compound, it was a nightmare. Most of the guards were doubled over, retching, faces twisted in agony. A few, less affected, gave the ambulance only a cursory glance before waving us through.

Price busied herself with hanging IVs and checking temperatures while Aaliyah and I wheeled the gurney through the front door. Inside was chaos—guards staggering, clutching their stomachs, some bolting for the bathrooms. The air stank of vomit, thick enough to taste. *Focus,* I told myself.

We passed a guard slumped over a trash bin. Aaliyah moved in.

"You doing okay, buddy?" she asked.

He barely shook his head before she pressed the cloth over his face. His eyes widened, then rolled back as he collapsed.

We pushed deeper into the compound, turning corner after corner until—there he was. The High-Value Person sat in a small room, flicking through TV channels, oblivious to the chaos. Confusion flickered across his face when we entered. When I drew my weapon from beneath the uniform, his expression hardened.

"On the stretcher," I ordered, keeping my voice steady.

He hesitated, lips curling into a faint, mocking smile—until I thumbed back the hammer. The click broke the stalemate. He rose slowly, lay on the gurney, his expression unreadable.

"Whiskey six-five-zero," I said into my comms, meeting Aaliyah's eyes. "Passing go, collecting two hundred."

Aaliyah gagged him and slipped an oxygen mask over his face while I strapped his arms and legs tight. He squirmed, but it was useless.

"Let's move," I said.

We were nearly out when the bathroom door swung open. A guard stumbled into our path.

"Hey! What are you—?" A cramp cut him short. He groaned, doubled over, and lurched back into the bathroom, slamming the door.

Aaliyah and I traded a wide-eyed look, then pushed through the front door to the waiting ambulance. The team piled in, doors slammed, Price behind the wheel.

"All set?" she asked.

I nodded, still half in disbelief. "All set."

The engine roared, sirens wailed, and as we sped away, I keyed my comms.

"We got him."

A cheer erupted in my earpiece. Laughter filled the ambulance. Even Price smiled, catching my eye in the rearview mirror.

***

Yeah, we got our kudos. And our Snickers bars. But what I walked away with was richer than any pat on the back or symphony of peanuts, caramel, and nougat cloaked in chocolate. I'd proven to myself that there was another way—one that *I* could choose, even in a place as rigid as The Program.

The person I most wanted to talk to about the mission was Eric. But when Sunday rolled around, he didn't show up to class. Aaliyah and I waited, our eyes fixed on the door long past the moment he should have walked in. A strange sense of foreboding tightened around me.

Almost an hour later, the wiry soldier who'd helped lead the Aikido sessions finally appeared. "He's not coming," he said, his words carrying a weight I could feel in my chest. "A drunk driver hit him last night."

"What hospital is he in?" someone asked, a faint spark of hope in his voice.

The soldier looked down, his face shadowed. "No, man... He's gone."

A cold fist seemed to close around my heart. He was gone, just like that.

For the rest of my time at The Fort, I found solace only in the movements of Aikido, each technique a tribute to him. With every turn, every breath, I could almost feel his presence, as if he were guiding me to keep learning, to honor his memory by carrying forward what he'd taught me. I made a quiet promise to myself: I would find my own way, like he'd shown me. I wouldn't let The Program or anything else decide who I am.

That night, as Aaliyah and I sat on our bunks, she nudged me gently. "Time's running out to choose your name, you know."

I looked at her, suddenly aware that this decision was more than a formality. It was the moment to honor a man who had changed my life. "Erica."

Aaliyah's face broke into a small, knowing smile. It was funny how much we could communicate in a single look by then—an understanding born of countless shared glances and whispered conversations in the dead of night.

Later, lying in bed, I felt a bittersweet mixture of loss and purpose settling over me. In the darkness, I whispered a quiet thank you—to Eric, to the universe, to the girl with the hearts in her window. They had all, in their own way, guided me toward balance in a world that seemed determined to tip the scales one way or the other and push me, pull me, define me.

After that, I applied Eric's lessons to every aspect of my life in *The Program*—and beyond. How I interacted with my teammates, how I handled the pressure to live up to crushing expectations, how I stood my ground without needing to push others down. I felt less like a puzzle of conflicting pieces, more like a complete picture—whole and unbroken, even if I was never quite finished.

Just over two hundred of us girls are moving on to the next phase. They've relocated us to an isolated former private school we've dubbed *The Farm*, where I'll spend most of the next three years of my life. Here, I can finally carve out a space of my own. My room—the first I've ever had to myself—is a cocoon, my small window framed by bright red curtains adorned with hearts, where I keep the dream of the life I once only imagined but am now creating, step by step.

E815

Part 1: The Severest of Schools

Every morning, E815 was the first to wake, slipping from his bunk to stand at the window and watch the sun rise over The Fort. As the first light spilled across the compound, a thrill stirred in him—a thrill that never faded. This place was sacred to him: the severest school meant to strip away weakness and forge someone new.

Outside the barracks, a massive black sign with gold letters greeted the recruits each day like a mantra. E815 knew the words by heart; they had changed his life the first time he read them:

We must remember that one man is much the same as another, and that he is best who is trained in the severest school.
— Thucydides

Most recruits walked past the sign with dread. Each day, the training got harder, the formations smaller, and those who remained did so with grim resolve. But E815 was different. He didn't endure The Program—he thrived in it. The grueling drills, the endless demands, the certainty that each day would push him to his limits—he loved all of it. Every morning, he felt himself becoming faster, stronger, more capable. The "why" didn't matter; only that he was shedding his old self, becoming someone who belonged here.

While others cursed under the weight of their packs or winced at fresh bruises from the obstacle course, E815 fought back a grin. It was as if The Program had been made for him. Every obstacle conquered felt like a triumph. This place was his symphony, and every muscle ache, every scraped knee, was part of its music.

Then the new trainers arrived—Navy SEALs—bringing drills that made everything before seem like child's play. The worst was the box drill. A black hood over the head. A dizzying spin until there was no sense of up or down. The hood yanked off. A burst of light, then one or two armed attackers rushing in. The recruit had to react instantly: disarm, disable, survive.

The first time E815 tried it, the light hit him like a punch. For a split second he thought he was ready—then he saw the flash of metal in his attacker's hand, and his mind went blank.

A glinting blade. A dim kitchen. His mother's knife catching the light.

Cold seized him. His chest locked. His limbs turned to lead.

"Strike! Do it, recruit! Strike!"

He could barely breathe. He crouched, arms over his head, as the SEAL instructor's voice cut through the panic. After a few seconds, they sent him to the back of the line. His heart pounded. His skin was clammy. The other recruits stared at the floor, oblivious.

What's wrong with you? You're supposed to be better than this.
But the memory still pulsed—the knife, his mother's face, the helplessness crawling up his spine.

He clenched his fists. *Get it together.*

The hood went on again. He swore he'd be ready this time. But when the light hit and the metal flashed, the memory came roaring back.

He froze. Arms up. Eyes shut. Heart hammering.

When he opened them, Chief Church was inches from his face, a glare hot enough to melt steel.

"Wastin' my time, Echo-Eight-One-Five?"

"No, Chief," he rasped.

"You froze twice. What are you—a head case? Or just a sissy?"

Shame burned hot in his gut. He could feel every eye on him.

"That's enough!" Master Chief Roberts barked from the platform. "Formation!"

E815 scrambled into line, but the shame stayed with him—raw and bitter.

                                ***

Twice a year, a man named Jack McBain had come to The Campus. Most times, he arrived without ceremony, watched the training in silence, and left the same way—his presence felt more than it was heard. But his first visit to The Fort was different. Halfway through the box drills, the whistle blew, and the Cadre lined them up so McBain could speak.

He was a tall, broad-shouldered man in his mid-forties, with the weathered face of someone who'd lived outdoors more than in. To E815, he was something between an idol and a god—someone to emulate, but whose existence seemed so removed from his own that he might as well dwell in some alternative universe. His combed back salt-and-pepper hair and eyes the color of storm clouds gave him the look of a man who had nothing to prove—a quality E815 envied the most. He carried himself like someone who knew exactly where he stood in the world, and that place was unshakable.

McBain's voice was calm but carried weight, the kind that made people stop fidgeting without realizing it. He announced that within the year, each recruit would be allowed to choose their own name—a rare flash of autonomy in a place built to strip it away. Then he named E253 as "Class Leader," which later prompted applause as they filed into the mess hall and E253 was seated at McBain's side for the meal, a place of quiet honor.

"They're ranking us," N960 whispered during lunch, breaking the ironclad no-talk rule. Violation meant the whole table paid: thirty pull-ups, sixty push-ups, ninety squats. They had all learned to read the Cadre's location, focus, and hearing range the way a hunter reads the wind.

E815 shot back, louder than he meant, his mood already sour. "So?"

"So... how many do they need?" N960's eyes flicked toward a cadre moving in their direction.

E815 pushed away from the table, leaving most of his food untouched, and bused his tray. But the question clung to him. Even if he conquered the hurdle in front of him, would it be enough? Would he be enough?

***

On Sundays, recruits could spend their time however they liked. E815 was one of the few who went to the local library, flipping through the battered catalogue of cassette tapes. His favorites were Bach and Corelli—music that felt like pure joy, clean and unbreakable. In the quiet of the listening room, he'd close his eyes and tilt his head back, letting the sound wash over him until it filled every corner of his mind. He listened until the melodies were engraved in memory, ready to be summoned when he needed them most.

He carried them everywhere. At sunrise, watching the first light spill over The Fort. Belly-down in the mud under barbed wire. Vaulting an obstacle wall. Driving through squats until his legs trembled and his breath burned in his throat. Even when the air around him was filled with groans, curses, and the slap of boots on gravel, Bach's precision or Corelli's warmth played on in his head.

"Come to the movies," his bunkmate, N960, said after their showers. Rocky IV was playing, and most of the recruits were going.

E815 glanced at his reflection in the dented locker mirror. Green eyes—his father's—had been a constant source of bitterness for his mother after he had abandoned them. Brown skin that had marked him as "spic" or "wetback" in every school he'd attended. A thin scar from his mother's knife. He couldn't erase them, but he dreamed of making them part of a self he could respect.

"I'm going to the bags," E815 said.

"Seriously?" N960 asked, pausing with a towel slung over his shoulder.

"Yeah."

N960 grinned. "I finally chose my name—Sipho. After my father."

"Good choice," E815 said. The smile didn't reach his eyes. Naming himself felt far away—like a privilege he hadn't earned.

The door swung open. Fortunado stepped in, tall, broad-shouldered, his gaze already locked on E815. Since the box-drill failures, his dislike had sharpened into something colder. Randall, his loyal shadow, trailed behind him.

"There's the class sissy," Fortunado said, his voice low but carrying.

E815's fists curled tight enough for his knuckles to ache. He kept his face flat. "Fuck off," he muttered, yanking a canteen from his locker.

"Yeah, go spank a monkey or something," Sipho shot back, mangling the idiom without flinching.

Fortunado's eyes narrowed. He stepped forward—just enough for the space between them to shrink—but stopped short. Everyone knew the rule: no fights outside sanctioned training. Anyone who broke it vanished.

"You should quit," Fortunado said, his tone dipping into a whisper meant to wound. "Before you get us killed. Chief Church says you're holding us all back. You know that?"

The name hit like a gut punch. Shame flared hot, tangled with something darker, something that whispered to hit him, rules be damned.

E815's breath slowed. He slid the canteen into his pack, turned without a word, and walked out. The humid air outside wrapped around him, heavy and wet, as if the whole compound wanted to keep him from leaving. But he kept walking, every step an act of will not to turn back.

***

He took the long way to the punching bags, letting the cool night air bleed the noise out of his head. Alone in the shadows, he allowed himself a break—just for a moment—his breath catching as heat pricked behind his eyes. He wiped it away fast, jaw tightening. Weakness had no place here. Not in daylight, not in darkness.

He rolled his shoulders back, squared to the bag, and brought his fists up. The first strike landed with a dull, satisfying thud. Then another. And another. The rhythm took over—measured, controlled—each blow a way to hammer down the things he couldn't afford to feel.

The "bag barn" was the only pool of light in a blacked-out sea, its pavilion throwing harsh shadows over the swaying rows of heavy bags.

Beyond it, the rest of the training grounds dissolved into darkness, the barracks barely visible between stray streetlamps.

On his first water break, E815 spotted a faint red glow near the road—a cigarette tip, most likely a Cadre on a late-night stroll n' smoke. By his second break, it was gone.

He cut back through the barracks, boots scraping against the gravel. Fortunado's voice still clung to him like smoke. Too tired to cry, he still couldn't shake the thought that maybe the instructors agreed.

"Echo Eight-One-Five." The voice was rough, like gravel under a boot.

He turned. The red glow was back, closer now—floating in the dark until a shape took form. An Army Sergeant First Class sat at a picnic table, cigarette between two fingers. Across from him was a recruit E815 didn't recognize.

"Yes, Sergeant," E815 said.

"Forget the 'sergeant' for a minute." The man flicked ash to the gravel. "Sit."

E815 slid onto the bench. The recruit's tag read E643. The Sergeant's nameplate: BLACK.

"You over at the bags just now?" Black asked.

E815 nodded.

Black pointed at him with the cigarette, smoke curling into the cold air. "Yeah... I've seen you before. Most days you look like a pig in shit out there." E815 almost smiled. "But tonight... you in a slump or suttin'?"

"Suttin'?" E815 repeated.

"Something," Black enunciated the word said with a dry chuckle. "You gotta learn Southern, recruit."

The air between them felt easier for a beat. Black crushed the cigarette out in a tin coffee can with come sand at the bottom.

"You pick your name yet?" E643 asked.

E815 shook his head. "Not yet."

"Me neither," E643 said.

"What was it before?"

Black lifted a hand. "Technically, you ain't supposed to share. But... hell, I've signed more NDAs than I can count. Go on."

"Dakota," E643 said reluctantly.

"I like it," Black said.

"I hate it," E643 muttered. "My dad was a junkie. After my mom left, I did everything—even scored for him. Couldn't even say my name right. Just 'D'koda,' like it was too much trouble to say the whole thing. 'D'koda! Get me a beer!'"

Black's head tilted. "Sounds like you sayin' 'Coda.'"

"Coda?" E643 asked, interest sparking. "That's a word?"

Black nodded. "Name of a Led Zeppelin album."

E643's face lit. "Zeppelin? Awesome!."

Black smirked. "You're gonna name yourself after a Zeppelin album? This is why they don't usually let y'all pick your own names." He turned to E815. "What about you?"

The name came out before E815 could think. "Jack."

Black's brows went up. "Jack?! As in the son of a—" He stopped himself. "The guy who runs this whole circus?" He gave a low whistle. "You must really want to be here."

E815 shrugged, eyes on the table. "I don't know if I'll be here much longer."

Black's cigarette paused halfway to his lips. "Why?"

E815's shoulders tightened. "Because... when the hood comes up in box drills, I freeze."

Black didn't flinch. "What do you feel when it comes up?"

"I... can't move."

"Fear?"

A reluctant nod.

"Fear of what?"

E815's voice dropped. "I think... I see my mom."

Black's tone softened. "What's ol' ma doing?"

"Slashing at me. With a knife." He mimed the motion, quick and sharp. "That's how I got the scar."

Black lit another cigarette and let the silence hang between them, the smoke drifting up into the night.

"Am I a... sissy?" E815 finally asked, on the verge of tears.

"Don't listen to Chief Church," Black said. "Not about that, anyway."

"Why not?"

"Because Church is doing something psychologists call projectin'," Black said, as if he knew the word firsthand. The two recruits looked at him, surprised to hear one of their instructors use what seemed to be a technical psychological term. "I'm takin' me some psych courses over at the college extension. Anyway, I'll tell you this—we're gonna fix your problem. You got my word."

"We?"

"Yeah." Black hooked a thumb toward E643. "*Coda* here's my ward on his free time, on account of sneakin' into town for a porno mag."

"Playmate of the Year," E643 (now Coda) said, half-proud, half-sheepish. "Totally worth it, even if I spent this afternoon sorting gravel by color, shape, and texture."

"Shut your piehole, you," Black said with a faint grin, then turned back to E815. "Now you're under my watch too. The three of us—we're gonna figure this out. Yes, sir."

Part 2: Jake

Every night that week, they came back to the bag barn. Black tried everything he could think of.

One night, it was breathing drills. "Slow it down," he told E815. "In through the nose, out through the mouth. Let the air do the work." Another night, he had him close his eyes before the hood went on, picturing himself landing each strike, over and over, until it felt second nature. When that didn't work, Black tried walking him through each step out loud during the drill, a steady voice in the chaos: *Turn. See the threat. Move your hands. Drive forward.*

It helped—barely. Some nights E815 lasted a few seconds longer before freezing. Once, he managed to land a single blow before the heaviness clamped down again. It was better than nothing, but the power wasn't there—not like on the heavy bags, where he could pour everything into every hit. Against a person, something in him still pulled back.

And Black knew it. E815 saw it in the way he'd stand there between runs, arms crossed, eyes narrowed—not angry, but searching for an answer he didn't have. The more they tried, the more the tension in his jaw seemed to set.

By Sunday night, all three of them were worn down. Coda and E815 sat on the sawdust floor, sweat cooling on their backs, while Black paced in a slow circle, cigarette in hand. Finally, he squatted in front of E815.

"You've got the tools," he said quietly. "But this thing's still in your way. And I don't think it's fear—not the kind you think." He held E815's gaze. "It's sadness. You said you see your mama with a knife. She slashed you with it and you don't know how to react, how to feel. So you don't react at all. You freeze. And I know why. 'Cause that was your mama, and she was supposed to love you."

The words landed like a punch. E815 felt them in his gut.

Black looked at the ground, embarrassed to admit the truth. "You're in trouble, kid. You need help, and you ain't gonna get it here. Trouble is, you ain't gonna get it out there, either."

Black sighed, looking older than he had all week. "I don't like what I'm about to say. But we've tried every other way I know. Tomorrow, if you freeze, they'll cut you. No more chances." He flicked ash into the sawdust. "So here it is—just for those moments, you've gotta feel nothing. Shut the door. Keep it all out. Go on autopilot."

E815 frowned. "Can I even do that?"

"Yeah," Black said. "I'd rather you didn't. But you're outta time."

***

Lying on his bunk hours later, E815 felt an unexpected calm settle over him. Knowing he'd be kicked out tomorrow brought a strange kind of peace, as if all the fight had drained from his body. It was like what he imagined a man on death row might feel in his final hour—dread lingering, but overtaken by acceptance. The struggle was done; all that was left was to wait.

Above him, Sipho's mattress creaked. A moment later, his up-side-down face appeared over the edge of the top bunk. "Still haven't picked a name?" he asked, keeping his voice low so as not to wake the others.

E815 managed a faint smile. "Doesn't matter now, but... Jack."

A snort of laughter came from across the room. Fortunado, pretending to sleep until now, broke into a cackle. "Ha! Because you're like a knockoff Jack!"

"Yeah... Would your middle name be Fake?" Randall chimed in, voice dripping with mockery. "Jack Fake... Jake for short!"

E815 let the laughter roll over him, untouched. He wanted to feel nothing, just as Black had told him. He wanted the mockery to bounce off him. If he couldn't... well, in less than a day, none of it would matter—Fortunado, Randall, even his name. It was all slipping away, and part of him almost welcomed it. He'd tried. He'd fought. Maybe he wasn't meant for The Program after all, no matter how much he loved it.

By morning, a heavy stillness hung over the barracks, as if even the walls sensed what was coming. E815 moved through his routine with numb detachment, brushing his teeth as if he were already somewhere else. He caught his reflection in the mirror and wondered who he'd be outside these walls, stripped of the purpose he'd held so tightly.

Sipho rinsed his mouth and glanced over. "Jake," he said, a hint of a smile playing on his lips. "You should think about it. Not a bad name."

Then he turned toward Randall, still snickering. "Better than Randall," he added, pronouncing it in such a pinched, nasal voice that even Fortunado chuckled.

***

Dread clung to him as E815 left the barracks. His stomach churned with each step toward the box-drill area, and when Chief Church's eyes pinned him, it was like a physical blow—tears pricked hot at the edges of his vision. *This is it,* he thought, gripping the thought like a lifeline. *One more failure, and I'm done.*

After grinding out his mandatory ten push-ups, he was given a latrine break. He headed straight for the last stall, farthest from the door, and sat down, elbows on his knees. He tried to breathe, tried to call up the calm from last night, but it was gone. All that was left was a low, gnawing fear that scraped at his ribs.

The bathroom door opened. He barely noticed—hydration was drilled into them, and people came and went all the time. But then... nothing. No footsteps moving past. No stalls opening. Just a silence that felt wrong.

The first hit came without warning—a violent *BANG* against the stall door that rattled the hinges and jolted through his chest. Then another. And another. Voices followed, close and sharp, circling him like wolves.

They didn't just shout—they hunted. Each word was aimed to wound, spat through the cracks, dripping with venom. Fists and boots hammered the door and walls, making the thin metal shudder. A shadow leaned over the top, and warm spit splattered his hair.

He shrank onto the toilet seat, curling in on himself, arms locked over his head. He tried to drown them out with Bach's clean notes, Corelli's gentle harmonies, but the music wouldn't hold. The noise chewed through it, tearing the melody apart until there was nothing left but the taunts, the smell of sweat and smoke, the pounding fists.

The laughter was worst—low and knowing, the sound of people who'd decided you were prey and wanted you to feel it.

So he stopped listening, and it was replaced with a deafening silence. His breathing slowed; his body went still. He waited until the fists quit pounding, the voices slipped away, and the door slammed shut.

He didn't know how long he sat on the toilet after they left—seconds, minutes, maybe more. Time had lost its meaning in the void in which he'd sheltered. When he finally emerged from the stall, he stepped up to the sink, washed their spit out of his hair, wiped it off his face, and blotted his uniform with paper towels.

He looked up into the mirror and met a pair of green eyes—cold, hard eyes that didn't flinch or waver.

When he exited the latrine, Jake strode confidently back to his line, his expression blank.

"Uh-uh," Chief Church's voice barked from the front. "You don't get to go to the end, Echo-eight-one-five. Front and center! Now, recruit!"

Jake snapped to attention, jogged to the front where Church waited, holding a black hood. He felt nothing—not fear, not anger, only an eerie calm. Even looking at Church, whose appearance and voice struck terror in him, he felt nothing—except, perhaps, a vague feeling of contempt.

"I'll give you a chance," Church sneered, his voice softening. "One chance. You can tell the Master Chief you quit. This life isn't for everyone. Maybe I was harsh because you need to realize your limitations." Raising his voice, he turned to the other recruits. "And you all need to understand that shortcomings like his can put you in body bags. Quit now, Echo eight-one-five."

Jake held Church's gaze, unmoved. The SEAL Chief's heavy breathing no longer intimidated him. It no longer even registered as a threat. Just a mild irritant.

"Fine." Church huffed, yanking the hood over Jake's head. "Everyone, gather around. Make a circle!"

Jake heard the shuffling of feet and the murmurs of the other recruits, but he didn't care. He closed his eyes under the hood and waited.

"I want all of you to see this," Church's voice boomed. "Because your lives will depend on each other's performance in the field. Watch!"

The hood came off with a sharp tug, and Jake's eyes snapped open, taking in the scene in front of him: a single attacker, knife in hand. Something—muscle memory, training, whatever—took over. He sidestepped, blocked the thrust, and grabbed the attacker's arm, twisting it with practiced precision. His right fist struck the padded recruit with enough force to make him double over. Without a pause, Jake seized the attacker's shoulder and drove his knee into the recruit's stomach. The recruit crumpled, gasping for air.

A medic rushed over, pulling off the recruit's facial padding. "He just got the wind knocked out of him," the medic said. But Jake saw the look in the recruit's eyes—shock tinged with fear.

"Bullshit!" Church roared. "You two, get over here!"

Jake glanced at two padded recruits as the hood enveloped him once more.

"The sun shines on a dog's ass some days," Church muttered. "Again!"

When the hood came off this time, Jake felt his body move without hesitation. He attacked the recruit with the gun first, wrenching the weapon from his grasp. When the second assailant lunged, Jake delivered a backkick to the groin, dropping him instantly. In a matter of seconds, he stood over both, gun in hand.

"I taught him that," Coda's voice rang out, breaking the silence.

As Church stormed off in a huff, the circle of recruits erupted into cheers. Hands clapped Jake on the back, fingers ruffled his hair, but he felt nothing—no elation, no connection. The adulation was good, and he acknowledged it with a smile and nod. But it was as if it wasn't for him at all. Something was in front of him, screening out whatever the others were sending his way.

***

The next time he saw SFC Black was Sunday night. Walking back to the barracks from the gym, Jake spotted the faint red glow of a cigarette in the area where they'd spent so many nights trying to conquer his fear.

"Sergeant Black," Jake called as he approached, his voice steady and detached.

Black turned, the cigarette glowing brighter as he inhaled. "Figured I might see you before I left," he said, his tone unreadable.

"You're leaving?"

"Yeah," Black replied, exhaling a cloud of smoke that drifted into the night air. "I've had enough. It's hard enough training seventeen- and eighteen-year-olds."

"Oh..." Jake paused, unsure of what to say. "I just wanted to thank you."

Black said nothing, his gaze fixed somewhere in the darkness. He took another slow drag, and the silence stretched between them. Finally, Jake broke it. "I guess you heard about... what happened in the drill."

Black's eyes shifted back to him. "I was there, kid," he said, his voice softening slightly. He stubbed out his cigarette on the bottom of his boot. "You're near the top of the class now. You're gonna make it... You're gonna make it all the way. How far that is, I don't know. But it don't matter. You'll make it."

A strange, hollow pride filled Jake's chest, and he forced himself to hold onto it, to keep it steady. "Do you... really have to leave?" he asked, the words escaping him before he could stop them. "It's just... you're a good teacher."

Black scoffed, shaking his head. "You don't know what you're talkin' about."

"I mean it," Jake insisted, his voice quieter. "I won't forget you."

Black was silent for a moment, looking at him with an intensity that made Jake shift, uncomfortable. Then Black's voice softened, almost too low to hear. "I know you won't," he said. "I just hope, one day, you'll forgive me."

Jake blinked, caught off guard. *Forgive him—for what?* But Black offered no explanation, only looked at him with a sadness that Jake couldn't quite place, a sadness that felt foreign and distant. Black gave him a last, lingering look, as if memorizing the face of the boy he'd tried so hard to save. Then he nodded and turned, walking away toward the parking lot, his boots crunching softly on the gravel. Jake watched him go, feeling a faint tug in his chest that he refused to name. He pushed it down, burying it somewhere deep inside.

Part 3: Silence

On a dark night in late December, clouds hung low and heavy over a mountain patrol base where Jake commanded forty recruits. It was the largest unit they'd formed since learning raids, and tonight's operation would be their final mission before the long march back to the barracks.

Jake just wanted to get it over with. They'd been outdoors for six grueling days. Two days earlier, rain had soaked them to the bone; then the temperature plunged, turning the ground into frozen mud. Now snow fell in thick, wet flakes, clinging to their uniforms and settling on the brim of Jake's patrol cap.

That morning, a fresh rotation of instructors had arrived to relieve the night crew. SFC Howard, clearly fresh from a warm bed, had stepped into the center of the patrol base, sniffed the air, and wrinkled his nose in theatrical disgust.

"Someone makin' Limburg fuckin' cheese out here?" he drawled, lip curling. "Y'all could knock a buzzard off a shit wagon, recruits! Y'all stink!"

TThe recruits cheered like it was the best news they'd ever heard.

Coda shouted back, "Your mom didn't seem to mind!"

That earned fifty push-ups, even though the cadre laughed as hard as the recruits.

SFC Howard then ordered an hour of "personal hygiene," making them change into their last clean uniforms. Even then, he still wasn't satisfied.

Jake was put in charge of the mission that day and he planned it as best he could, eager to get everyone moving again to fight off the biting cold. He set a brisk pace, pushing past his own exhaustion and hunger. By the time they reached the edge of the compound, there was still just enough daylight to get a clear look.

From the reconnaissance photos, Jake knew the layout: two lookout towers and a barracks—his planned targets. But as he and Sipho crept up the hill, they saw something new. A coil of concertina wire now ringed the entire perimeter. The only way in or out was a checkpoint, guarded by a machine gun nest.

"Even if we take the towers and the guards, that gun will cut us down before we can get close," Sipho whispered, his breath curling in the cold air.

Jake's jaw tightened. The chill had sunk deep into his bones, dulling his thoughts. Command didn't make him less cold, hungry, or tired—it only made the problem heavier.

SFC Howard, listening in, raised an eyebrow. "Well now, recruits," he drawled, "you've got yourself a pickle, don't ya?"

Jake's mind raced, but the fog of fatigue made every thought sluggish.

"Hey..." Sipho whispered. "Remember about three hundred meters back? We passed some plywood. What if we laid a sheet of that over the wire?"

Howard grunted. "Not bad, recruit. But it won't be heavy enough. You lay that on top, it's just gonna bounce and flop around. You need somethin' to weigh it down."

"Rucksacks," Sipho offered.

Their massive green packs carried everything—cold-weather clothes, ponchos, paracord (which they were learning had a thousand uses), hygiene kits, and other essentials, all packed tight in waterproof bags. They were heavy enough to dread after a single day of marching, let alone six.

Jake glanced at Sipho, a small smile forming on his lips. An idea sparked through the haze of fatigue.

"I have a better idea," he said, voice low but sure.

***

Snow was falling hard when Jake radioed his machine gun teams to initiate the assault. Two M60s, positioned high on the hill above the compound, took turns hammering the entrance. Even with blank adapters fixed to the barrels, the "pig" lived up to its name—each

BAP-BAP-BAP-BAP-BAP cracked through the forest, muzzle flashes strobing the dark trees and falling snow.

As the compound's defenders returned fire and swung floodlights toward the hillside, Jake's assault team slipped through the dark woods to the western perimeter. Less than two hours earlier, they'd built the weapon he'd conceived on the fly. Fortunado was now its centerpiece—wedged between two large sheets of plywood, bound tight with bungee cords. He looked absurd, like the filling in a plywood sandwich. His expression was twisted with discomfort.

At Jake's signal, Fortunado drew a deep breath and hurled himself belly-first onto the concertina wire. The coils bit into the plywood and sagged under his weight, forming a crude bridge.

One by one, the recruits dashed across him, boots thudding on the boards as he grunted and winced beneath them. Jake crossed last, looking down at Fortunado's flushed face—humiliation and pain were etched in every line. *This is where you belong,* Jake thought.

Fortunado's open contempt had been replaced by wordless compliance. Jake felt a grim satisfaction as they cleared the wire, breached the compound, and seized their objective.

***

A few hours later, they gathered in a university dining hall transformed for Christmas Eve. Garlands looped along the walls, holiday centerpieces brightened the tables. McBain, visiting for the second time that year, sat at the head table with Jake to his right—a seat of honor.

A string quartet played Corelli as they dined. The familiar strains should have lifted him, the way they had on those quiet Sunday afternoons in the library, headphones on, eyes closed, letting Bach's clean strings or Corelli's warm harmonies flood his mind until they became part of him. Back then, the music had been armor—something pure and unbreakable he could carry anywhere. He'd played it in his head at sunrise, the notes lifting him above the grind, or under barbed wire in the mud, steadying his breath while the world pressed down.

Now, sitting just feet from the musicians, he felt... nothing. The sound seemed trapped behind glass, each note muffled.

Around him, recruits laughed, swapped stories from their final exercise, and speculated about what came next. Jake stayed quiet, wearing a polite smile, feeling only a faint pride in his accomplishments and a vague disdain for the noise. Across the table, Fortunado caught his eye and—unexpectedly—offered a faint smile and respectful nod. Jake ignored him.

But even here, at the head table, with peers looking up to him, a hollowness gnawed at him. Pride faded quickly, replaced by the cold, familiar anxiety of needing to stay ahead. Failure wasn't an option. Anything was better than feeling shame again.

Corelli played on, thin and lifeless, a sound he could no longer reach. The notes that had once soared inside him now felt distant, thin, as if bouncing off unseen walls.

When training resumed, he went back to the music room, slipping on his headphones as if they might take him back—back to that sunrise over The Fort, Corelli threading through the light, back to the bag barn where each punch landed in time with the music in his head. For a moment, it almost worked. But when the music stopped, the emptiness returned, leaving only the cold grind toward the next task, the next goal. Pride and shame were all that remained; everything else was blurred by the numbness that had settled inside him.

He thought of those old melodies, of the joy they once stirred, and felt a flicker of something—an ache he couldn't name. He buried it before it could grow, letting it sink into the distance. In the end, all that remained was pain and the absence of pain.

The music was gone.

THE BULLY

Part 1: Playmate of the Year

I was never religious, but I think I've spent more of my life doing penance and seeking forgiveness than most Christians out there—especially those who judge people like me and then tell me, "Oh, *I'm* not judging you. *God* is judging you." That's usually when the part of me that I've worked so hard to kill reminds me that it's still there. It's the part that hates. What does it hate? You might as well be asking Johnny Strabler what he's rebelling against (look it up—you won't regret it). The list is long and banal.

I meet a lot of people who were in *The Program* who didn't make it all the way through—who "failed" even if I hate using that word. I meet them because I make it my business to see them and provide help if they need it. Most dropped out in Phase 2, when things went from downright punishing to brutal.

Back then, for all I knew, I was the only gay boy on the planet. It didn't make any sense. Of course, it didn't. But who knows anything when they're 13, and who doesn't think they know everything at 13?

Understand that I worshipped at the altar of (what I thought was) masculinity. I was from a family dominated by men, acting the way they thought a man was supposed to act. Maybe if I'd been smarter, I would have abandoned machismo when my mother wound up in the ground and my father behind bars. Maybe I wouldn't have taken his name – Fortunado.

The Program was a test of manliness, at least as I saw it. Not the kind of manliness Jack McBain embodied—he was a distant, godlike figure, too abstract to be real. It was the SEAL cadre who arrived at The Fort that brought masculinity into sharp, gritty focus. Chief Church, especially. Church was big, loud, and brimming with swagger, his voice booming across the sawdust pits and hangars where we trained. He had a belly, sure, but he was mostly muscle, bluster, and a whole lot of attitude. He wore shorts so tight we called them "ball huggers," and he had a SEAL trident tattooed on his thigh. The guy was practically a walking ad for testosterone supplements.

So, yeah, I had the biggest crush on Chief Church. I wanted to be him. I wanted *him*. I was disgusted with myself that I wanted to be with him, mostly because I thought *he* would be disgusted if he knew what I wanted.

Maybe you think how I felt about him was my first "sin." You'd be wrong. Even if I wasn't gay, I was barely a teenager. It's a confusing fucking time. No... "sin" is when you do something that's you know is wrong because it makes you feel better about yourself. When Church picked Jake out of the recruits and taunted him for freezing up on those box drills, I knew that piling on was wrong. But Church had given me a purpose and a focus beyond keeping my secret and staying in the program, and that was to make Jake quit. Because, most of all, I wanted to purge from myself the weakness Church saw in Jake. I wanted Church to *see* me as I wanted to him to see me. I wanted his approval, his aknowledgement that I was worth something.

***

Some of the people from The Program—the ones who didn't make it—ask me, *"When did you know you were gay?"* I figure they're curious because, in their eyes, I never did anything "gay" while they were there with me.

So I ask them when they realized they were straight.

It's never one moment. It's like becoming an adult—a slow, creeping thing. You don't notice it happening until you look back and realize you're not sure what was real and what just happened in your head, like a dream you're still half inside.

So, no—I don't know *when* it was. But I remember the moment I couldn't pretend I was the same as everyone else.

At The Fort, I shared a room with Randall, Sipho, and Jake. In another life, I might've been friends with Jake. We were both Latino. My family is Mexican, though nobody there knew it. Even after I chose my name, people assumed I was white—too fair-skinned for them to think otherwise. Jake was half Puerto Rican, half white, with a darker complexion than mine. You might think that wouldn't matter—and it shouldn't—but in the U.S., skin tone is its own kind of prison. We discriminate, exoticize, envy, loathe—all over the shade of someone's skin.

I didn't want anyone connecting me to my background, so I kept my distance.

On Sundays, I usually played soccer with the other recruits. That's where I met E643, who'd given himself the name "Coda" after a Led Zeppelin album.

Coda had that dangerous sort of charm—the kind that could make trouble sound like an adventure. He wasn't the smartest of us, but he was clever in a way that could get you caught up in something before you realized the risk. I figured it'd get him kicked out sooner or later.

One Sunday after a game, he pulled together a small knot of recruits and pitched his latest stunt: sneaking into town to get a Playboy.

No civilian clothes? No money? No personal property allowed? Coda had an answer for everything.

"We'll cut through the woods," he said, grinning like it was already a done deal. "We'll wear PT gear—we'll look like any other kids."

"Other kids don't wear matching shorts and T-shirts," I said.

"They do if they're on a soccer team," he shot back without missing a beat.

"Where exactly are we going?"

"There's a gas station three miles away."

It was more like five, but Coda had a flexible relationship with the truth.

"How do you know?" Sipho asked.

"I found it," Coda said. "I even went inside. The guy at the counter was Russian."

"Why were you there?" I asked.

"I got lost during land nav."

He grinned wider, like he knew exactly how far to push and just how much to leave unsaid. And that was the thing about Coda—half the time you didn't know if he was bluffing, and by the time you figured it out, you were already in the game.

But most of us bowed out. I mean—would you follow a guy into the woods to find a place he stumbled across while getting lost?

"Dude, I totally know where it is," he insisted to the handful of us who stayed.

"Even if we find it," Sipho said, "we don't have any money."

Coda glanced around the field, eyes lit with mischief. "I got something to trade."

"What?" I asked, incredulous. You have to understand that everything we owned was meticulously accounted for. Lose something, and you'd be writing a long paper on how it happened, maybe spending your free time searching for it before it was replaced. Then they'd probably make you tie it to yourself with paracord—which, along with "hundred-mile-an-hour tape" (duct tape), was about the only thing we had in abundance. So whatever Coda had was contraband—that was, if he had anything at all. Either way, he wasn't going to tell us unless we agreed to go.

***

Me and Sipho were deep in the woods with him before Coda finally showed us. From a little leather pouch, he pulled out a multi-tool that looked like a Swiss Army knife but was way cooler. It even had needle-nose pliers with a crimper!

I read the name on the case: *Leatherman.*

"I think you should forget the Playboy," Sipho told him. Coda was busy working the compass. "You should keep this."

"No way," Coda said. "If the Cadre saw me with it, they'd confiscate it and give me two hundred push-ups or something."

"If they catch you with a Playboy, it'll probably be worse," I pointed out as we climbed over rocks and fallen trees.

"Yeah, but this way, I'll at least get something out of it," Coda replied.

"Like what?" I asked. "They're gonna take the Playboy just like they would take the Leatherman."

"Well, *obviously*," he said. "But to *use* the Leatherman, I have to *have* the Leatherman. I don't need the Playboy to use it."

I must've looked confused, because he tapped his temple. "Dude, I just need to see it once. After that, every time I get to look at it again is a bonus—because it'll all be up here. In my spank bank. I can use it whenever I want to rub one out." He made the universal sign for male masturbation.

"How did you say it?" Sipho asked. "Rub it out?"

"Rub *one* out," Coda corrected him. "Yeah. You know... spank the monkey."

"Monkey?"

"It's a saying," I told him. "For jacking off. Spank the monkey. Like flog the dolphin, or... beat your meat."

"Jack your beanstalk," Coda added. "Burp the worm." He stopped, looked at Sipho with mock gravity, and said, "Manhandle... the ham candle."

That one got me laughing so hard my eyes watered. And it started a little tradition that lasted almost our whole time at The Fort. However miserable things got—cold, wet, exhausted—if one of us came up with another euphemism for masturbation, it got us through. Juvenile? You bet. But it made life a little more bearable.

Sure enough, after what felt like hours of stumbling over roots and weaving through thickets, we came out of the woods practically on top of the gas station. It appeared so suddenly through the trees that we froze, like deer stepping onto a road. The last thing any of us wanted was to blunder straight into the open and get spotted by someone who'd start asking questions.

We crouched behind a rotting log, watching. The place looked sleepy enough—a gas pump island and the faint hum of a soda machine outside—but there was a pickup parked off to the side.

"Could be the guy who works here," Coda whispered.

"Could be someone who calls the cops if they see three kids in matching shorts creeping around," I muttered.

We waited until the sound of a passing car faded down the road before circling wide, sticking to the shadows. Every crunch of leaves underfoot seemed too loud. At one point, we flattened ourselves against the cinderblock wall as another truck rumbled past, the driver glancing our way without slowing.

On the far side, Coda stopped, scanning the lot like a burglar. "Looks clear."

"You're sure about this?" Sipho asked.

Coda grinned. "Relax. I got this."

He slipped the Leatherman into his hand like a gambler palming an ace and ducked through the glass door, the little bell above it jingling loud enough to make my stomach tighten.

Sipho and I retreated to a gap in the tree line where we could keep watch. Through the window, we saw him leaning on the counter, talking to the man inside—bald, heavyset, wearing a flannel shirt. They chatted like they knew each other. The man laughed at something Coda said, and I tried to guess whether that was good or bad.

Then Coda disappeared down an aisle. My mind started running through all the ways this could go sideways: the guy refusing the trade, calling the cops, confiscating the Leatherman... or worse, phoning The Fort. Ten minutes in the real world felt like an eternity.

Finally, Coda reappeared at the register. The man bent down, produced a brown paper bag, and slid it across. Coda stuffed it under his arm, gave a casual wave, and pushed through the door like he'd just bought a pack of gum.

Only when he was back in the shadows with us did I exhale. His grin was pure triumph.

"The guy gave me last month's issue," Coda said. "But there's good news... Gentlemen, I give you Playmate of the *Year*, Ms. Kathy Shower."

There she was—one of the sexiest women alive (supposedly), all glossy and airbrushed, with boobs and teased hair practically jumping off the page.

And I felt nothing.

For a terrifying moment, I thought my lack of reaction might make me suspect—but Coda and Sipho were too busy committing the images to memory to notice. When it was my turn, I took the magazine to a spot where they couldn't see me, and read a very interesting interview with Kareem Abdul-Jabbar.

Part 2: Fear and Loathing

Coda was caught almost immediately. Contraband like that wouldn't stay hidden for long. I almost wished he'd ratted us out—at least then the others might think I was straight. But he kept his mouth shut.

One night soon after, I lay in the dark, listening to my roommates twist in their bunks, the bedsprings groaning with every turn. My stomach was knotted tight, my skin prickling with heat. I think I knew who I was then. I could still lie to myself for now, but I knew what anyone else would think if they caught one whiff of what was inside me. I could almost see my father's face in the shadows, the embodiment of machismo, glaring down at me with the kind of contempt that could cut you to pieces. I could almost hear him spit the word for what I was—low, foul, final.

Then, a soft chirp. An alarm. None of us had clocks; we didn't need them. The Cadre made sure of that, usually with something loud and violent—a garbage can hurled into the hallway, a door slammed hard enough to rattle the frame. But we all had G-Shocks. I'd never heard one go off before, but I knew the sound.

I kept still, feigning sleep, and watched through half-lidded eyes as Jake stirred in his bunk above Sipho. He swung his legs over the edge, sat there in the dim pre-dawn, and stared out the window at the thin band of orange light creeping over the trees. He looked... peaceful. Like he belonged. Like the world made sense for him in a way it never had for me.

It wasn't envy of what he owned. It was envy of his *existence*.

The next day, the SEALs arrived. Soon we were in the pit, starting the box drills. And then there was Church. I was drawn to him instantly, but what hooked me was the moment he pointed at Jake after the second time he froze in a drill. Church spat a single word at Jake—sharp, cold, contemptuous: *sissy.*

That was the spark. All the disgust I carried for myself leapt onto Jake like it had been waiting for a place to land. In that moment, he became the weakness, the softness, the thing to despise.

And I enjoyed making him feel it.

I couldn't touch him—fighting would get you thrown out—but I found other ways. I made a smile just for him. Not a friendly one. Not even openly cruel. Just enough to let him know I *knew*. In the pit, during drills, in the mess hall—if our eyes met, I'd give him that grin. A little private signal.

I know what you are. I decide what you are.

I didn't think Church saw me at first, but I wanted him to. I wanted him to see that I wasn't like Jake. That I was sharper, harder, more worthy. And maybe—just maybe—he did notice. The way his gaze flicked toward me when Jake faltered again. The way he didn't tell me to stop. Maybe he even recognized a piece of himself in me.

God help me, I hoped so.

***

Then came the day we all expected Jake to get kicked out.

That morning, I told myself I felt nothing but anticipation—but it wasn't true. There was a twist of something else in there that I didn't want to name. On one hand, my contempt for him was about to be endorsed by the people whose approval I craved most. On the other, I knew I'd be losing something—a living outlet for everything I hated in myself. Without him, where would it all go?

I watched him at the back of the line, shoulders hunched, trembling. Part of me wanted him to collapse right there. Part of me wanted him to hold out, so I could keep chipping away at him.

He slipped into the latrine, and that's when Chief Church called me over.

"You want that sissy with you when you go into some heavy shit?" he asked.

"No, Chief," I said. My voice was steady, but inside, I was a live wire. Being this close to him was intoxicating. If he sensed it, he didn't show it.

"Take a few recruits," he told me. "Go in there with him and do what you need to do. When he comes out, I want him to walk right up to the Master Chief and quit. You hear me?"

It was *The Karate Kid* moment—Kreese telling Johnny to *sweep the leg*. But unlike Johnny, I didn't hesitate. This wasn't a tournament. There was no such thing as fair play here. And if there was, I didn't want it.

I gathered a few recruits. Some hesitated. Others smiled the way jackals do when they smell blood. Sipho was the only one who flat-out refused. He didn't give a reason, but I took it as a choice—a choice for Jake, against me.

Randall and the others followed me inside. The air was thick with the smell of disinfectant and old piss. My footsteps echoed as I walked to the stall. I could see Jake's shadow under the door, his boots planted like he was trying to stand firm.

We hit him all at once. Shaking the door. Kicking the panels. Spitting over the top. Shouting until our voices bounced off the tile and came back at us warped and ugly. My own voice didn't even sound like mine. It was deeper, harsher.

I wanted him to quit. I *needed* him to quit. Not just for Church, but so I could believe the thing I'd been telling myself: that he was weak, and I was strong. That whatever he was, it had nothing to do with me.

I kept pounding until my fists stung. Until I was sure I'd driven it home. Until I believed—really believed—that when that door opened, Jake would be finished.

***

So... yeah. That didn't exactly go how I thought it would. We broke Jake and fixed him at the same time. He got over whatever caused him to freeze, and he was one of the golden recruits after that. I half expected him to get me back, and maybe we'd call it even—patch things up in the unspoken way recruits sometimes did. But he never did.

The closest he came was on a mission we ran on Christmas Eve. He had me do a body breach through concertina wire, then sent about thirty recruits charging over me to take the objective. Fine. Fair enough. I could respect that.

I waited for him to rebound after that, to shake it off and go back to being that kid who got up early just to watch the sunrise every morning. But he never did. That light in him I'd once envied never came back.

Oh, yeah... You might wonder how I knew it was Christmas Eve. After the mission, they brought us to this huge dining hall at a university and had this great dinner all laid out for us. It was like nothing any of us had ever seen. The girls were there, too. We'd lost so many that we thought they must have taken some to another place. Then we got two days off in a row to just hang out in the dorms and rest.

But I had a hard time sleeping. It was at night that those thoughts crept back into my head.

The dorm was silent, the other recruits just faint shapes in their bunks, the occasional creak of a bed frame or rustle of blankets the only signs of life. Outside, snow was falling thick and steady, muffling everything in a thick white hush. Through the window, the streetlights glowed softly against the snowflakes, casting long, pale lines across the walls, so faint they were almost ghostly.

I lay on my back, staring up at the ceiling, feeling the slow thud of my heart against my ribs. It was so quiet I could almost hear it echo in my chest, each beat too loud, too fast. I tried to focus on my breathing, to steady it, but it just made me more aware of the tightness spreading through my chest. I felt this strange ache... something like longing. Longing for what? A part of me didn't even know. The silence of the campus outside, the emptiness, felt almost too vast, pressing in on me, filling the room with a weight that felt like it was settling into my lungs. My pulse was a rapid, insistent drumbeat, too fast, too loud, and the harder I tried to calm down, the more I felt it spiraling out of control.

I shifted onto my side, pressing my face into the scratchy dorm pillow, squeezing my eyes shut as if that could block out everything clawing its way to the surface—every ugly, hateful thought. I saw my father's face, sneering, disgust twisting his mouth. *Maricón.* That's what he'd call me. Like he'd always known, like he could see something I'd tried so hard to bury.

I turned onto my back again, breathing too fast, feeling my fingers clench into fists, cursing this weakness inside me. But lying here, with nothing but my thoughts and that awful silence, I felt like a scared kid again. I told myself that I didn't belong here. I didn't belong anywhere.

I sat up suddenly, unable to lie there any longer, my pulse pounding in my throat. The air in the room felt too thick, too stale. I needed to move, to breathe.

Sliding off my bunk, I grabbed my PT jacket from the foot of the bed, pulling it over my T-shirt as quietly as I could, not wanting to wake anyone. The cold hit me like a slap when I stepped outside, but I welcomed it, letting it sting my face, letting it pull me out of the spiral.

Outside, snow was falling in thick, lazy flakes, gathering in soft drifts along the empty sidewalks. The campus lay deserted, a wide, white silence stretching in every direction. For a long moment, I just stood there, watching it collect on the bare branches, the world impossibly still.

I closed my eyes and drew a deep breath, the cold air filling my lungs. For a second, I almost felt calm—almost felt like myself. But the ache returned, sharp and insistent. Being out here wasn't enough. Breathing wasn't enough. The hollow place inside me remained.

I thought about running—about carving a path through the snow like I had as a kid, not stopping until my legs gave out, the cold in my chest chasing everything else away.

The stillness seemed to deepen, the snowfall whispering against the ground. I felt suspended there, alone in that white quiet—until I heard the faint click of a door latch behind me.

I turned my head slowly. Sipho stood in the doorway, hands buried in his jacket pockets, watching me with that quiet, knowing expression he always seemed to wear.

"You couldn't sleep either?" he said—more a statement than a question.

"I, uh…" I glanced back out at the fresh blanket of snow stretching into the darkness, avoiding his eyes. "What are you doing up?"

"You know how Jake snores," he said, a grin tugging at his lips.

"I still can't believe he picked that name," I said, shaking my head. We both chuckled softly.

We stood in silence, watching the snowfall, until the words I'd been choking back for three months finally broke free. "I don't think I belong here."

"Why?" he asked.

I didn't answer.

"You named yourself for your father—same as me," he said.

"Yeah. That's right." I was startled by how much regret bled into my voice.

"Where is he?"

"Prison. He… killed my mother because he thought she was having an affair."

Sipho nodded, a quiet acknowledgment. "I'm sorry."

"What about yours?" I asked.

"He died," Sipho said, his gaze dropping. Then he looked up, met my eyes, and said, "I killed him."

I froze, my mouth half open, no words coming out. I must have looked like an idiot.

Sipho sat down, leaning back against the cold brick portico wall, and let his head rest there, eyes half-closed.

"I'm from Nhambalale," he said. "A tiny village in Mozambique. We had a small farm, some chickens, and goats. We knew there was a civil war, but it felt far away, like something happening in another world.

"One day, the rebels—the, um... Resistência Nacional Moçambicana—came to Nhambalale. I was seven. For reasons I'll never understand, they came straight to our farm. They wanted to take me as a soldier. They said if I didn't go with them, they'd kill my whole family.

"I said I would go. But that wasn't enough—they wanted proof of loyalty. They told me I had to kill either my brother or my father. If I refused, they'd kill them both."

"Jesus," I breathed.

"The last thing my father said to me was *ungalahlekelwa ubuntu bakho.*" Sipho's voice caught as he spoke the Zulu words, and tears began spilling down his cheeks. He wiped them away roughly, sniffed, cleared his throat.

"It means something like, 'Don't let them make you an animal.'"

"I'd guess this is the last place you'd want to be," I said.

Sipho shrugged. "This place is different. Not so different that I'll stay. I'll finish The Program, go to college... but I won't kill for them."

"You think they'll keep their word and let you go?"

He nodded once. "And I'll go back to Mozambique. I'll find my brother."

I just stared at him, stunned. Every recruit had a hard story, but I was pretty sure Sipho's was the worst I'd ever heard. Still, he carried it with a kind of quiet strength that left me in awe.

It didn't make my problems feel petty exactly. This was the 1980s, and being what I was didn't exactly fly in a place like this. Still, standing there in the snow, my own burden felt... lighter. Not gone. Not shared. Just a little less crushing—for the moment, anyway.

"I'm going to try to get some sleep," he said. "You coming inside?"

"Yeah," I said.

"And if you go back and can't fall asleep, try boxing the one-eyed champ."

"What?"

He laughed and said, "Punch the clown!"

"Oh! You mean rough up the suspect! Because you know he's guilty."

To this day, I love those masturbation euphemisms.

Part 3: The Cold

It was cold—that's the first thing I remember about where they sent us next. Not the kind of cold you just feel on your skin, but the kind that seeps into your bones and waits for you to make a mistake. Our shelters were flimsy, more symbolic than useful, but we weren't meant to spend much time in them anyway.

The place could be beautiful—frozen lakes and rivers stretching to the horizon, mountains sharp against a glassy sky... like a Bob Ross painting. But even then, you could feel the edge under it.

The instructors said we were training to fight in extreme cold—the kind you might find in certain parts of the Soviet Union. The problem, looking back, was that hardly anyone in the U.S. was an expert at it. The regular military planned to fight in Europe, mostly with vehicles. What we were trying to learn was something almost no one had ever thought through.

At first, it almost felt like a vacation. We learned to ski—both downhill and cross-country—and how to move over snow with snowshoes and snowmobiles. But soon we were running the same drills we'd done at The Fort, only now we were learning how the cold could grind down both us and our enemies.

That morning started bright, with sunlight flashing off the snow so hard it stabbed your eyes even through ski goggles. But the light felt too sharp, the air too still. Then the change came.

Clouds slid over the mountain like a lid closing on a box. The wind started high and distant, then dropped on us all at once—howling down the slopes like a wild animal. A wall of gray swallowed the sky, and in moments, the world around us was gone.

The temperature plunged, and the wind hit like a fist, tearing through our layers as if we were standing there in nothing but T-shirts. Snow whipped around us, stinging every scrap of exposed skin, turning the air into a swirling, blinding chaos.

"Recruits, keep moving!" one of the Cadre bellowed, his voice barely carrying over the wind. "Stay with your unit!"

We were racing down the mountain, trying to get back to the shelters. I couldn't see more than a few feet ahead. Every step was a gamble—you never knew if your boot would hit solid ground or sink into a hidden drift.

I kept my eyes on the recruit in front of me, but he was little more than a shadow in the whiteout. My heart pounded from the effort of pushing through the snow, but at first, I wasn't afraid. We'd been in bad situations before, and the Cadre had always pulled us through.

Then came the order to ditch our rucksacks and sling our rifles. They'd never told us to do anything like that. That's when the fear set in.

Voices called out around me—muffled, distant—but I couldn't tell who they belonged to or where they were coming from. The storm felt almost intelligent, slamming into us from different directions, driving us apart. I tugged at my balaclava, but the wind clawed at my face, burning my cheeks before numbing them completely.

The recruit in front of me—I don't remember who it was—went down. I hauled him back to his feet, but we'd already lost sight of the person ahead of him. My heart jumped into my throat as we pushed harder, and we nearly slammed into the back of the line. Relief washed over me—until I glanced back.

Behind us, there was nothing but gray haze.

"Coda! Sipho!" I yelled into the whiteout, but the wind shredded my voice before it could carry. It was pointless—nobody could hear me. Coda had been behind me, I was sure, and I thought Sipho was behind him.

Then something slammed into me from the side, hard enough to stagger me. I spun, half ready to swing, and saw Chief Church. Behind his goggle lenses, his eyes were wider than I'd ever seen them.

"Where's the rest of the squad?" I shouted, my voice rasping from the cold.

"I don't know!" he barked back, but the pitch was wrong—too sharp, too fast.

"You didn't pass them?"

A quick shake of the head. No explanation.

"Don't worry!" he called, already angling his body forward, unwilling to stand still. "There's a cadre at the rear! Keep moving!"

For a second, I just stared at him. In the tilt of his head, the tightness around his mouth, I saw something I'd come to recognize over the years since—fear dressed up as certainty. We were all scared, but behind me, in that roiling wall of snow, were my friends.

"I'm going back!" I shouted.

He didn't answer—just shoved me forward. "Keep going! That's an order!"

I planted my feet and turned, but this time his shove knocked me into the snow. I braced for him to lean down and rip into me, to threaten me with being thrown out. Instead, his boot brushed my balaclava as he stepped over me without looking back.

By the time I scrambled up, he was gone—just another shadow swallowed by the storm.

I was alone.

I began backtracking, eyes locked on the fading footprints, my only guide through the blur of white.

Then came a sound that didn't belong to wind or storm—a deep, rolling growl, so low I felt it before I heard it. At first I thought it was my imagination, but then the snow under my boots gave a faint vibration. The growl swelled, spreading through the ground, the way thunder rolls through your bones. It was the sound of something impossibly big waking up.

And then it roared.

Not the snow itself—not yet—but the voice of it. A freight train in the sky, barreling straight at me. The wind snapped and shifted, slamming into me from a new angle. The ground trembled harder. Then the snow moved—not falling, but rushing, pulling at me like it wanted me with it.

I lost the trail instantly. My feet slid out from under me, and I went with it, tumbling and skidding in the cold rush. I didn't know it until later, but I was right at the edge of the avalanche. Maybe if Church hadn't knocked me down earlier, I would've been in the center.

When the movement stopped, there was nothing. Just silence. The kind that presses on your ears. I sat there for—seconds? minutes?—my breath rasping inside my balaclava, heart pounding like it was trying to break out of my chest.

A shadow appeared through the haze—one of the Cadre—who hauled me to my feet and steered me back toward the shelter.

Before the storm was even over, they had us on the mountain again, hundreds of us spread across the slopes with entrenching tools, digging. The storm had stripped away every landmark, leaving a frozen maze of blank white horizons and half-buried shapes. Recruits and Cadre alike crouched low against the wind, hacking at drifts, their shouts carried and broken by the gusts. Every so often a voice would call out a number, sharp and urgent, vanishing into the storm before you could tell where it came from.

The cold gnawed at my hands as I tore at the snow, each scoop burning my skin before the numbness set in. My gloves were soaked, heavy, and useless against the frost, but I didn't care. All I could think about was Sipho and Coda—trapped somewhere beneath, frozen in the dark, faces locked in fear.

"Fortunado!" a voice shouted, faint over the wind, but I kept digging. The snow wasn't soft; it was packed and unyielding, more like ice than powder. My fingers cramped, my shoulders ached. Every breath came in short, ragged bursts, steaming up my goggles until I could barely see. Still, I clawed deeper, convinced they were just inches away.

"Fortunado—over here!" The voice cut sharper this time.

I looked up to see one of the Cadre waving from a few yards away. He was kneeling over something—someone—and my stomach dropped.

I stumbled toward him, my legs heavy, the world narrowing to that single point in the snow.

It was Coda. Half-buried, his face chalk-white, lips tinged blue—but his chest rose and fell in shallow, stubborn breaths. The Cadre was already clearing the drift from around him, the snow clinging to Coda's clothes in thick sheets.

I dropped to my knees and dug beside him, my hands shaking as I freed his arms and legs. The snow resisted every movement, clinging and refreezing in the cold air.

"He's hypothermic," the Cadre muttered, breath clouding. "We need to get him back to the shelter—now."

I couldn't speak. My throat felt locked, my heart hammering too hard. I just stared at Coda's slack, colorless face, willing him to keep breathing. My hands hovered over him, useless, until the Cadre's rough grip clamped down on my shoulder, jolting me.

"Focus!" he barked. "Help me lift him!"

We hoisted Coda onto a makeshift stretcher—a tarp strung between two poles—and began the long, punishing haul back to the shelter. The snow dragged at our boots, the wind clawed at our faces, and every step felt like it stole more strength. But I kept moving, the weight of the stretcher nothing compared to the desperate need to get him inside.

By the time we reached the shelter's perimeter, a new sound cut through the steady hum of the diesel generators—a low, rhythmic thump growing louder. The recruits had cleared the helipad, and a medevac helicopter came in hard. Farther off, the taillights of other choppers hovered in the dark, circling, waiting their turn to land.

We handed Coda over to a pair of medics. I was still catching my breath when another stretcher emerged from the storm.

At first, all I saw was a bundle of blankets, a pale face half-hidden, an oxygen tube taped in place. Then the stretcher drew level with me, and the world seemed to tilt.

It was Sipho.

***

We lost Sipho and a Cadre from the SEALs. Coda made it, but he was never really the same. None of us were.

We buried more than two people that week. We buried pieces of ourselves.

The night they told us Sipho was gone, something in me cracked wide open. All the shame, guilt, and fear I'd been carrying poured out in a way I couldn't stop. I cried until it felt like my body was trying to wring out my soul—and then, just like that, I was empty. After that night, no matter what happened, no matter how much I wanted to, I couldn't cry again.

Sipho was the first friend who made me feel like I was a good person. He didn't know all my secrets, but somehow he sensed the weight I carried and never judged me for it. And he wasn't "soft," not in the way Church used the word as a weapon. Sipho wasn't weak. He was stronger than any of us, and kind. There's a difference—a difference I didn't understand until that Christmas Eve at the university.

I used to think masculinity was what Chief Church embodied: the loud voice, the swagger, the will to dominate. I thought courage meant being unshakable, unflinching. Sipho showed me something else. He had every reason to hate the world, to harden himself into something unbreakable. But he didn't. He chose to carry his humanity, even when it hurt. Especially when it hurt.

And then there was me. I didn't lift people up—I put them down. I put Jake down because it made me feel better about who I was. I bullied him because I hated the parts of myself I saw reflected in him—the parts that were vulnerable, scared, not enough. I thought if I could make him suffer, I wouldn't have to feel my own pain. But now I feel certain that Sipho saw right through me.

After the funeral, we started greeting each other the way Sipho taught us in Zulu.

Sawubona. I see you.

Ngikhona. I am here.

It became our ritual, our way of holding onto him. And maybe, for me, it was a way of holding onto something I'd buried deep inside myself—something I didn't want to lose. Because that's what Sipho taught me: to see people, truly see them... and to let myself be seen in return.

I stopped trying to be like Church after that. Stopped trying to prove I was something I wasn't—I still had my moments, still lashed out when I felt small—but Sipho's voice was always there, steady and soft. *Ungalahlekelwa ubuntu bakho.* Don't lose your humanity.

Jack McBain didn't come to the funeral. That stayed with me for years, a stone lodged deep inside. At the time, I told myself it didn't matter. McBain was an abstraction—a distant god, cold as the place Sipho had died. What difference would it have made if he showed up?

McBain didn't *see* us. Not really.

We saw each other.

Melissa

Part 1: Disbanded

Light spills softly through the blinds—the pale, early-spring kind that carries no warmth, only a thin shimmer across the floorboards. I don't move. I just lie there, watching dust wander through the slats like tiny, aimless ghosts.

In that gray space between sleep and waking, it happens. Not always, but when it does, it's here. I breathe in, and suddenly he's beside me again—the smell of his skin, the warmth of his breath. I know it's a trick of the mind, like catching sight of someone you've lost in the blur of a crowd.

And then the moment's gone. It always goes.

The apartment is silent. My roommates are scattered—Miami, Montreal, wherever people go to feel free.

This was our bed, once. Not in the literal sense—he never lived here—but we spent whole weekends in it, folded around each other, hiding from the world as if it couldn't breach the fragile shell we'd built. The sagging mattress didn't matter, nor the heat clanging on in the middle of the night. When he was here, the room was a sanctuary, and something in me felt like it was mending just from the sound of him breathing.

Two years ago—his senior year, my sophomore. Now I'm the senior, staring down another choice.

I told him I couldn't do long distance. That was the lie. The truth was simpler, and worse: I couldn't keep pretending. He loved a version of me I had stitched together for him—the sweet, clever girl who listened to his stories and made him feel seen. I was good at her. I didn't mean to deceive him. I just didn't know who else to be.

Sometimes I wonder if there's anything under the stitching. If I peeled it all away—the smiles, The Program, the grades, the careful little victories—would there be anyone left? Or just an empty shape where a person should be. The silence where something was meant to grow and didn't.

I roll onto my back, eyes tracing the ceiling. A thin crack runs from the light fixture to the wall. I've meant to report it for years. I never have. It hasn't spread. It hasn't healed. It just exists.

I miss him the way you miss something that was never really yours. I think he knew I loved him. I wonder if he still loves me.

Enough.

***

Eight hours on the Amtrak to Boston. I could've flown—would've been there in a fraction of the time, hugging my siblings before dark. But the truth is, aside from the time I spent with Greg that year, these were the hours I treasured most: the ones I got to be alone. Not alone-alone, obviously. But with a good pair of headphones, a

Discman, and a case full of CDs—enough armor to keep any seatmate at bay.

The Bends went in first. I'd probably play it again before Union Station in D.C. Maybe after Hootie and the Blowfish.

Mostly, I watched the window. March was still winter south of Boston—gray trees, gray sky, gray earth. Even the snow seemed tired of itself, reduced to crusted, dirty piles slumped against curbs and corners, unwilling to admit it was supposed to melt.

Every so often, I looked up—not to speak, just to see.

Across the aisle, a mother with a daughter who couldn't be more than six. Coloring books spread open, juice boxes sweating on the tray table. The mother leaned in to whisper something, and the girl's shoulders shook with silent laughter. I tried not to stare, but there was something in the way she leaned back into her mother without thinking, like it was the safest place in the world. My chest tightens even now. Not jealousy. Just... the hollow ache of watching a scene from a movie I was never cast in.

Farther down, a couple curled into each other like matching book-ends. They'd split a pair of earphones—one over each ear—and the girl was tracing her thumb over the guy's knuckles in a slow, absent loop. I used to do that with Greg. I never knew if he noticed. He probably did. He noticed everything, especially when I was slipping away.

A few rows ahead, a group of college kids. Their laughter rolled over the seats, punctuated by the crinkle of a Skittles bag and the fizz of Mountain Dew bottles. One girl wore a hoodie from a school I'd visited once but never applied to.

I leaned back and played "Fake Plastic Trees." Closed my eyes.

The train rocked and hummed beneath me, a cradle with a crooked lullaby, whispering that everything here in this car is everything I'm not.

***

The train hissed to a halt. The platform blurred past the window.

Union Station.

I slung my bag over my shoulder and folded into the flow of passengers. The air outside hit me—heavy, humid, already tasting of pavement and exhaust.

Then... a twinge at the base of my neck. A prickle along my shoulders, like static finding ground.

I didn't ignore that. No woman should. Especially not a recruit.

I kept moving. Eyes forward. My thumb eased the volume down on my headphones. The rest of me stayed loose, casual.

Reflections in the glass. Flickers at the edge of my vision.

Someone was keeping pace.

Ten feet back.

Too close. Wrong rhythm.

Could be nothing.

It's never nothing.

I blended into the crowd, then cut left toward the terminal stairs. At the last second, I pivoted—looped through a Hudson News, pausing just long enough to pretend I was deciding between gum and tabloids.

Slipped back out. Crossed to the other side. Escalator up two levels. Down one.

Still there.

Dark hoodie. Aviators. Pale denim. Posture all wrong—trying too hard to be casual.

I slid my hand inside my jacket. The Glock's grip settled into my palm like an old friend.

Behind a column. Count to three. Double back.

Fast. Low. Silent.

Gun low, angled. Not drawn. Not yet.

"Turn around," I said. "Slowly."

He froze. Turned.

Scottie.

Hoodie pulled tight, aviators reflecting the station lights, and a mustache so fake it was probably still warm from the glue.

He grinned like a game show host caught cheating.

"Jesus, Mel," he said, "you almost shot me."

"Why the fuck are you dressed like the Unabomber?"

Then I heard it—that sharp, wheezy laugh. Coda stepped out from behind a trash can, doubled over and red in the face.

"He made me do it," Scottie said, pushing back the hood and sliding off the sunglasses. How had I missed that sandy-blond hair? He'd tucked it in well.

He peeled off the fake mustache. "We even practiced the walk. She wasn't supposed to see me."

"You're both idiots," I said—but I was smiling now.

I let them hug me. Even Coda, who smelled like Dr Pepper and Polo.

By the time the shuttle came to pick us up, there were six of us ready to go. And for a couple of hours in a van headed to some facility in Virginia where we'd stay the week, we were just six college seniors on the verge of graduation. No talk of training. No rumors about being disbanded.

Because we weren't some of the most highly trained intelligence operatives in the world. We were college kids. We told stories about parties, sex, sports. We blasted songs and screamed the lyrics at the top of our lungs.

And I loved them—my brothers and sisters. This was the only life I'd really known. Life in the pressure cooker of the Program. As painful as it had been, it had made me strong. And I belonged.

***

The room was half theater, half lecture hall: a sloped floor, rows of fixed seats, and a broad stage framed by curtains that looked like they hadn't been drawn in years. The air carried that institutional smell—old air, warm plastic, and something faintly chemical. The ancient sound system coughed with static now and then, as if clearing its throat.

Nearly six hundred of us were crammed in, knees against backs, shoulders touching. The last time we'd been here was years ago, when most of us were fifteen or sixteen. We'd been smaller then—and quieter. Now, with college ending and the Program winding down, if anyone hadn't caught senioritis yet, it was spreading fast. Laughter. Shouts. Hugs.

I sat dead center, next to one of my favorite people—Fortunado. Tall, broad shoulders and chest, with a mane of hair it was hard not to run your fingers through. Of course he was gay. Beautiful men were either gay or complete assholes.

We hugged.

"Sawubona. Sup, sis?"

"Ngikhona," I replied.

He tipped his chin toward Jack McBain, standing by the steps to the stage with the other Program Director, Rohan Khan.

"Think they're doing it?" he asked. "Disbanding us?"

I shrugged, though I didn't believe it. After so many years—so much money, pain, even death—and all the talk about how vital we'd be, not just to America but to the world... disbanding us made no sense.

"What will you do if it happens?" he asked.

Before I could answer, McBain climbed the stairs. The room stilled. He moved to the podium without looking up, papers in one hand, jaw set hard. The mic squealed, then cut off with a pop. He adjusted it anyway. There was more gray in his hair now, deeper lines in his face.

He ran through the courtesy script—welcome back, good to see you, all that—and then:

"Most of you know the Program has been under review for some time," he said. "The administration has decided not to go forward with it."

The reaction hit in a wave—sharp exhales, half laughs, half gasps. Silence followed, but it was brittle.

A chair creaked near the front, slow and high-pitched. Someone muttered *no* under their breath, the sound of reality tilting. Paper rustled—a page dropped, a pen fell, a notebook snapped shut.

Then the whispers. Not gossip—shock. Raw, involuntary: *What? Are you serious? This can't be happening.* They moved through the room like wind in dry leaves.

Stillness settled. Not calm—impact. Like after a car crash, when nothing moves but nothing feels still.

McBain cleared his throat. "Believe it or not, this has happened before."

He swept a finger across the room. "You're all Janissaries now. For those who don't know, they were elite soldiers in the Ottoman Empire. Taken as boys, trained hard, broken harder. Yeah... a bit on the nose. I didn't name us."

A few chuckles—thin, uncertain—floated through the air.

"The idea was simple," McBain continued. "Train elite operators the same way we train elite athletes and world-class musicians: start them young, and push them until they're as capable as human beings can be. There was only one other class before you—mine. Mine and Rohan's. Now there's you."

He paused, looking out over us, letting it soak in.

"This happened to me and my brothers in '78," McBain said. "We knew it could happen again. So we prepared for it."

The lights dropped.

The curtains drew back as *Also Sprach Zarathustra* rumbled through the speakers. Cheesy as hell. At the music's peak, the screen came alive: a diving eagle, talons spread, frozen in the instant before the strike. Beneath it, a Latin motto burned into view—*Aut inveniam viam aut faciam.* Then the name: **JANISSARY SOLUTIONS, OG.**

By the time the last note faded, Rohan Khan was standing beside McBain.

"We're creating a company unlike any other in the world," McBain said.

A ripple moved through the rows—side glances, slight shifts. We'd all known something was coming. Just not this.

"We'll be based in Vienna and operate across the globe, doing what we've been trained to do for the last fifteen years. We'll ride the wave of outsourcing and take this company—and ourselves—to new heights."

He stepped back, let the promise hang, then leaned in.

"You've been trained in the dark. Taught to think, to adapt, to finish what others can't even start. While the world was distracted by wars it didn't understand, we were building something better. Smarter. Leaner. Now the world's changing—and it's finally ready for people like us."

A few heads nodded. Small. Careful. The kind of nods that meant: *I want to believe you.*

"Governments are stepping back. Markets are stepping in. Intelligence, security, special operations—it's all being privatized. Quietly. Steadily. Irreversibly."

He paused. Tapped the podium once.

"We won't fight the tide."

Another tap.

"We will be the tide."

It landed. A low murmur rolled through the room. Someone in the back exhaled, sharp and long, like they'd just understood the offer on the table.

"Janissary Solutions will be our vehicle. You'll have autonomy. Flexibility. Pay that matches your worth." He ticked the words like a checklist. "No red tape. No pretend oversight from people who couldn't survive the first week of your training. You'll answer to your team, your clients, and yourselves."

The room sat in the in-between—tempted, skeptical, processing.

McBain stepped forward.

"Some of you are angry," he said. "Confused. You think the Program was your purpose. That this is some kind of betrayal."

He planted his hands on the lectern.

"Let me be clear. This is the next phase. Not a compromise. A liberation. We're not shutting the doors—" he leaned in "—we're kicking them open."

A few rows ahead, Cecilia stood. "You want us to become mercenaries?" she asked. Her voice was worn thin.

A low rumble rolled through the room. Agreement. My gut twisted. She was saying what we were all thinking.

McBain didn't blink. A slow shake of the head. "Not mercenaries," he said. "Contractors."

"What's the difference?" someone called.

He lifted a hand, palm out. Steady.

"Mercenaries fight for money alone. Contractors serve a purpose. We choose which contracts are worth our time. That's the difference. We won't take orders from the highest bidder. We'll pick our battles. Our clients. Our causes."

The words settled. Then his tone lowered—steadier now.

"I know you're angry. You were told you'd serve something bigger than yourselves. So was I. But meaning isn't found in bureaucracy or politics—it's found in the work. In the people beside you when it counts. That's what I'm offering."

The silence after wasn't empty. It was dense. Tension, disbelief, dread, hope—braided so tight I couldn't tell which thread was mine.

"The Program is done," McBain said. "That's fact. We can scatter. Let the system break us apart. Pretend this never happened."

A pause.

"Or... we stay together. We take everything we've built—the skills, the loyalty, the blood we've spilled—and carry it forward.

"Janissary Solutions isn't just a company. It's ours. Our structure. Our teams. Our rules. This is how we stay in the fight. This is how we stay with the only family most of us have ever known.

"You want to know what matters most? This is it. Staying with your brothers. Staying with your sisters. The ones who stood with you when you were nothing—when no one else would.

"You walk away now—you lose that. You come with us—" his hand cut the air "—we stay together."

The Program had been everything to me—my mission, my family, my life. I'd loved it and hated it in turns, but it was always there. Always with me.

We had until the end of the week to decide.

Part 2: Scars

The next day, they handed us our personnel folders, each one topped with a Top Secret cover sheet and sealed with a little sticker you had to break to open.

"The only other copies will be kept on magnetic tape in a secure facility," McBain said. "If you're joining Janissary Solutions, hand it back in. Otherwise, they're yours to do with as you see fit."

So that was how much they wanted us to vanish—not even a line in an active database. Just a reel of tape, the kind used to store Cold War secrets.

I took mine to a quiet spot at our little getaway site—a man-made pond with a paved walkway and a few benches.

W248. It had been years since anyone called me that. The sound of it pulled an unexpected smile from me. It had been even longer since anyone used my real name. There it was on the first page: *Pamela Swint.* Birthplace: Twin Falls, Idaho. That was news to me. We were living in Colorado when I was recruited. Then again, I was so young, maybe I was remembering it wrong.

Scottie stood nearby, looking out at the still water, his folder tucked under his arm. I loved Scottie. Everyone loved Scottie. He was funny, he was sweet, and the guy could sing and dance like nobody I knew in real life. The others still talked about how, back in Phase 2, the cadre would have him sing whenever there was a delay. He knew dozens—maybe hundreds—of songs by heart, and he loved performing.

"Learn anything about yourself?" I asked him.

He smiled. "Nah. I was just about to turn it back in."

"You're staying, then?"

He nodded and sat beside me, the folder resting in his lap. That's when I noticed the seal hadn't even been broken.

"You're not even going to open it?"

He shook his head, squinting at the sunlight glinting off the water. "One of the reasons I picked Juilliard is because it's in New York," he said. "That's where I'm from."

"Really?"

"Yup." He glanced up with a faint smile. "It was just me and my mom. She was beautiful, you know? Young, looking back on it. We lived in this loft I always remembered as an artist's dream—full of color, music, people drifting in and out like they belonged to some shared story. And my mom, she was a dancer.

"We walked past a *Nutcracker* poster once, and I just stopped. Couldn't take my eyes off it. The Sugar Plum Fairy was right there in the center, and I asked if that was what she did. She nodded. 'Yeah,' she said. I believed her completely.

"I'd ask if I could see her dance, and she'd always say, 'soon.' Soon. We'd dance together sometimes—'Crocodile Rock.' You know that one?"

"Of course," I said.

"Yeah, we had this whole routine..."

"Do you still remember it?"

"A little..."

He stood, humming the tune, swaying his hips in a half-choreographed shuffle. It made me laugh—not because he was messing it up, but because it was exactly how you'd picture a kid imagining a routine.

He sat back down, and the smile slipped away.

"I thought she was shot in a mugging," he said at last. "One day she was there. The next..."

"Sounds like she really loved you," I said—because nothing else felt right.

He nodded. "But there was so much I didn't know about her. Ten years later, I went to New York, tried to find that loft, those people. But everything I remembered was gone. I dug a little more, and..."

He stopped, tapping the folder. "I know what this is going to say. That my mother had me when she was fifteen. That her stepfather was my biological father. That her own mother kicked her out, and she squatted in an empty factory in Brooklyn with a lot of other runaways. It'll say she worked as a stripper in Hell's Kitchen until my father found her, shot her, and then himself."

"Jesus..." I murmured.

"I don't need to see these papers," he said, lifting the folder. "Because I decide who she was. I decide what we were. No one else will remember her. So I want her to live up here, in these memories—real or not. Not in this stack of paper."

He held the folder like it was something alive, something venomous. He wasn't shaking, but there was a tightness in his jaw, a weight in his eyes that hadn't been there a minute ago.

I thought of Greg—the way he used to look at me, like I was something rare and steady. Like I made sense.

But I wasn't. I didn't. He didn't really see me. Like Scottie, he saw what he wanted—a beautiful illusion.

And yet I can't help wondering... did I get it backwards? Was Greg's love real, and I was just too afraid to see it? Why would I be afraid? Or was he in love with someone who never existed—just as Scottie's mother only lives in that one perfect moment, dancing in a loft that was never really theirs?

***

At night, we drank and talked and laughed. No doubt some of us were hooking up, though it had always been strictly against the rules in the Program.

During the day, we played soccer and volleyball—forgetting, for just a little while, the decision hanging over us.

After dinner, the beer and liquor flowed through the living quarters like an enormous frat party. I sat with Cecelia and Fortunado in a room that could've passed for the cheapest suite in the cheapest hotel chain—bare walls, thin carpet, and one sad chair that Fortunado had claimed.

The door was open, so people drifted in and out, or paused in the hallway to wave or say hello. There was no shortage of conversation that night.

Fortunado surprised me. He was never the top recruit, but far from the bottom. Still, you never really knew who drank the Kool-Aid and who just learned how to play the part.

"I was going to leave after college, anyway," he said.

"Why?" I asked.

"I don't think you can do this stuff and keep your humanity. Not for long, anyway."

He leaned forward, elbows on his knees, hands clasped like he was holding something fragile.

"It's not the danger. You brace for that—you train for it. But it's the in-between that rots you. The way you start scanning people the way you'd scan a street—angles, exits, threats. You stop seeing faces. You see variables. Problems to solve, assets to use, obstacles to move."

He shook his head slowly. "Last year, I was walking through the city and saw this homeless guy outside a bodega. Middle of winter, hands like cracked leather, lips blue. And I didn't think, *poor guy*. I didn't think anything. My brain just filed him as obstruction—adjust route. It was clean. Efficient. Cold.

"That scared the shit out of me, Mel. More than any op. Because in that moment, I realized I'd lost the reflex to care. And once you lose that..." He trailed off, gaze shifting to the open door as laughter drifted in.

"I don't want to be one of those guys who can only function in the dark. Who start needing the dark."

He leaned back, tapping the chair arm twice, a restless rhythm. "I was never the best. You know that. But I kept trying. And somewhere along the way, I realized that the more I 'improved,' the less I liked the person I was becoming. And I think I'm done trying to be the kind of person who's good at this."

"I know how you feel," Cecelia said, sipping the beer she'd been nursing. She was next to me on the bed in a tank top and shorts, catching the eye of every guy who passed the door. We were close—like siblings, in a way—but no one had six hundred 'siblings' so close they wouldn't sleep with any of them. And Cecelia... well, she was lethal. Like a Latina Barbie with a switchblade smile and a body built to make trouble.

"But I think I'm going to go," she said. "I mean... fuck it. What else am I going to do?"

She twirled the beer bottle between her fingers, staring at the label.

"I've got a degree no one outside the Program cares about. No résumé I can actually show anyone. I could spend the next year waiting tables and pretending I'm working toward something, or I could take the one offer on the table that uses what I'm good at.

"I like the work. Not all of it. But I like being good at something that matters—at least to the people I'm doing it with. I like the rush, the focus. I like knowing exactly where I stand and what I'm supposed to do. Out there in the 'real world,' no one gives you that. It's just chaos, and I don't think I'm built for it anymore.

"So yeah. I'm going to try. Maybe it'll chew me up. Maybe I'll hate myself in five years. But at least I'll know I didn't walk away from the only thing I've ever done that made me feel... like I belonged."

From the hallway, we heard one of the drinking songs we'd co-opted over the years. The verses always changed in this one, but the chorus stayed the same.

Drink, drank, drunk last night,
Drunk the night before,
Gonna get drunk tonight
Like we never got drunk before!

'Cause when we are drunk we're as happy as can be,
For we are all now Janissaries!
See Janissaries are the best that can be,
And no one can out-drink the likes of we.

Not the Highland Dutch
Nor the Lowland Dutch,
The Rotterdam Dutch,
Or the other damned Dutch!

Glorious! Victorious!
One keg of beer for the four of us.
Glory to the gods there are no more of us,
'Cause one of us could drink it all alone!

Jake appeared in the doorway. He'd been using a bit of makeup lately to dull the scar on his left cheek, but it still showed. We were so used to seeing it, it was hard not to look for it. He'd always hated it.

He'd also never really liked Fortunado—but that didn't matter. He ignored him, and me. Jake ignored most people, but Cecelia always got his attention.

He greeted us, though his gaze was already locked on her. "Sawubona. I like your toenails," he said.

"Thank you," she replied, smiling up at him. It was easy, practiced—just enough to play along, not enough to promise anything.

Fortunado and I exchanged a glance. Then he excused himself, slipping past Jake, who stepped in and took his seat.

"CIA's coming tomorrow, if anyone's interested," Jake said.

"They're recruiting?" I asked.

"Yeah. Six billets." He took a sip of beer. "Something called the Special Activities Division."

"Are you going to apply?" Cecelia asked.

He shrugged. "Depends."

"On?"

"Are you?"

She laughed—half flirtation, half boredom. She knew his attention was like weather—bright one moment, dull the next. He matched her tone perfectly, both of them keeping it light, transactional. I was almost disappointed we didn't get the Jake laugh—an awkward, closed-mouth one-note sound that rose and fell without warning. Everyone had their own impression of it.

"I think I'll pass," she said, idly twirling her ponytail. She was humoring him, but I could see it in her eyes—she knew better. Jake's interest in her, in anyone, was a short-term game.

He grinned. "I didn't want to work for something called SAD anyway."

"This is just a job," Cecelia said. "A very intense, very dangerous one... but I think I can still have a life and do it."

"It might even be fun," Jake said, a devilish grin tugging at his mouth.

"Erica!" Cecelia called, and I glanced toward the doorway to see Erica pop her head in.

"Sawubona," she said.

Cecelia waved her in, and she dropped onto the bed beside me.

"Five-oh," Cecelia said.

"Five-oh," Erica echoed, and they bumped fists.

Erica caught the puzzled look on my face. "Our team number," she explained.

"Say *my* team," Cecelia told her.

"You're the leader?" I asked Erica.

She nodded—too humble to say it aloud.

I wasn't surprised. Everyone loved Erica. If I'd had to pick a team leader straight out of Phase 3, it would've been her. Even back in Phase 2—when most of us were still trying to prove we were tougher, faster, louder—Erica never played that game. She never shouted. Never postured. But when she spoke, people listened. And when something went wrong—a jammed rifle, a teammate puking from heat exhaustion—she was already moving, already fixing the problem before the rest of us had even processed it.

In Phase 3, when the missions turned more cerebral, she only got better. She ran surveillance like she was born for it. Read situations faster than the instructors. But more than that—she read people. Not just their tells or their weaknesses, but the currents underneath: the fear, the ego, the need to be seen.

She never humiliated anyone. She never had to. She just made you want to do better.

"Georgetown's on a roll," Jake said, referring to the university from which he and Erica were both about to graduate.

"You're a team leader?" Cecelia asked.

"Janissary Twelve."

Jake was good. No one denied that. Precise, sharp, surgical. He executed like he had something to prove and no intention of failing. He studied harder than anyone, trained longer, hit every benchmark with an intensity that made instructors take note. On paper, he was what the Program wanted. Maybe even what it was designed to produce.

But leadership? That was different.

Jake didn't lead so much as perform leadership. He issued orders with the confidence of someone who was sure he was the smartest person in the room. Even if he was, you never got the feeling he saw the rest of us as people. Just assets. Pieces on a board.

He took input like it was an inconvenience. He delegated well enough, but there was always a subtext: *You're only doing this because I let you.* And if someone else shone too bright, Jake dimmed the lights. Not overtly. He was too polished for that. But you felt it.

People followed him because he was efficient. Because disobeying Jake meant walking into a wall of cold, professional disappointment, and no one wanted to feel small under that glare.

Of course they made him a team leader.

He couldn't tolerate being anything else.

"What I want to know," Cecelia said, leaning toward him, "is if there was ever a point you thought of quitting."

"Oh yeah," he said. Both Cecelia and I drew a sharp breath at the same time before laughing at how perfectly in sync it was. That got the Jake laugh—finally. But Erica didn't seem surprised at all.

Cecelia asked her why.

"Because I saw it," Erica replied.

"So something happened at Georgetown," I said, and now we were all looking at Jake.

"All right, fuck it..." He set his beer down, like it was the only way to make himself keep talking. "I met this girl a couple years ago. Things got serious."

"Name," Cecelia said.

"Isabel."

"Latina?"

"Of course." His mouth twisted into the faintest grin—it was his type, the reason he liked Cecelia, or at least looking at her. She blushed, just a little.

"I loved her... like, fiercely," Jake said, leaning back in his chair as if to give the memory space. "I actually started to believe in God for a while. Because I thought—there's no way someone so... made for me just shows up by accident. I mean, I could've gone to another school. She could've been twenty years older, or born twenty years from now. So it couldn't have been an accident. Right?"

His voice had changed—lower, unguarded. I'd never seen him like this. I think it was how I must have looked when I talked about Greg.

"I would've quit," Jake said. "Didn't care. I could drive a truck or flip burgers, as long as I had her."

"What happened?" I asked.

"I don't know, exactly." He rubbed his jaw, gaze sliding toward the floor. "Maybe I'm not the easiest to talk to."

Cecelia and I exchanged a look—*understatement of the year*—but we didn't want to interrupt. Jake was just tipsy enough to open up, just enough to let something real slip through.

"I knew I wanted to be closer than we even were," he went on. "I just... I didn't know what to do when she was sad or angry. I didn't even know what to do when she was happy."

He turned his head toward the window but didn't seem to see it. "She just... pulled away. She graduated. Moved back to California. And after she was gone, I couldn't believe it. Like maybe I imagined it all."

"I met her, Jake," Erica said quietly. "She's real."

"I mean how she felt about me." His eyes flicked toward us—quick, almost defensive—then back to the window. "If it was ever real. I always wondered why they supervised us every second growing up, and then just let us loose in college. I think it was another test. But we decided what it'll be, and it's the hardest one. She was mine."

He stopped, breathing through his nose. His voice dropped even lower. "Funny thing is, I don't know where this one ends, you know? She still haunts me. Everything I do, I'm thinking... is this making me more or less worthy of being with her? It's like she's watching, just out of reach. But all I feel is judgment. None of her warmth. No passion. Just judgment.

Not good enough."

The last three words were barely audible, spoken into the blank space in front of him.

As he passed by later, I caught a glimpse of the makeup covering the scar on his face. And I realized why he did it. He was filled with scars, just like the rest of us.

And he was wrong—about it not being real, about it being just a test. These memories, these traumas, these unresolved feelings we don't know what to do with—these ghosts—they're real.

I used to think I was insulated against them, or that I would be again once college was over and I was operating with my siblings. But there he was, the best of us by almost any measure, and he could be the most haunted of us all.

Part 3: Ghosts

The week is nearly over. Teams have formed. Tattoos have been inked.

Erica and I are sitting on the roof of our temporary dormitory, watching the boys—eighty percent of the class after The Fort—wandering the cold country air, burning their files and God-knows-what else in rusted barrels.

She turns to me, her nose ring catching the glow of the fires. "What are you going to do?"

"Why?" I ask with a crooked smile. "You got a spot for me on Five-Oh?"

"Engineer," she says. "If you want it."

It's tempting. I love Erica. I love the other girls on her team. We'd be good. Very fucking good.

"I can tell Jake's story about Izzy really tripped something in you," Erica says.

I nod.

"So you got serious with someone," Erica says. "You're human, Mel. Even Jake got his heart broke, and who knew he even had one?"

We laugh, but it collapses under the weight of what's inevitably next.

"What happened?" she asks.

"I dumped Greg."

"And why did *we* dump Greg?" she asks.

I lift my head and wipe at my eyes. "Did you just use the royal *we?*"

"We did indeed."

We clink our beer bottles together and take a sip. I glance down at the yard—at everyone and no one in particular—and wipe my nose on my sleeve.

"I thought it would be easier to leave than get left."

"You thought if you told him about The Program, he'd dump you."

"I thought if he saw who I really am..." I stop, because the words nearly break me. I choke back most of the tears, but a few escape. I've never said it out loud before: *If he saw who I really am...*

Erica nods knowingly. "Sounds bad when it comes out like that, doesn't it?"

I nod through the tears, and she puts her arms around me again. I tell her about Scottie's mom.

"I just wish I could be like him," I say. "Just have good memories and forget all the dark shit."

"How do you remember your mother?" she asks.

"I don't. There's just this blurry blank space where a mother should be. You?"

"Same," she says. "No wonder we're so fucked up, right?"

We clink bottles again and drink, but my mood isn't improving.

"I don't want to feel this way anymore," I tell her. "If I go with you, I think... maybe—not right away, but eventually—I could forget him. Just like I forgot my mom and everything else that hurt me in The Program. I'd have to, just to survive."

"Maybe," she says. "But forgetting isn't the same as healing. If you can live with that, then sure—come with me."

***

The doors groaned open, and I stepped out with my duffel over my shoulder and the folder in my hand. For a moment I just stood there, savoring the warmth of the spring sun on my face. Around me were all my brothers and sisters, gathered in one place for the last time.

The courtyard had become a crossroads. To the left, clusters of recruits pressed shoulder to shoulder, handing in their packets and falling into neat five-person teams. Their laughter carried across the air, sharp and bright, edged with adrenaline.

To the right, buses idled with their windows open to let the breeze in. A few faces already watched from behind the glass, framed like portraits in another life. Others stood at the base of the steps with bags at their feet, murmuring last words before climbing aboard.

Between them, the burn barrels glowed dull orange in the morning light. Smoke rose in slow threads, thick with the smell of ash and scorched paper. One girl tore a page at a time, feeding it in like she could ration the letting go. Two guys tossed whole folders into the fire, laughing as the flames flared.

Everywhere I looked it was goodbye and persuasion: *Come with us. You'll regret it. Don't be stupid.* But people had had all week, and their minds were set.

The air hummed with it—affection, fear, defiance—all tangled together, louder than any cadre ever was.

I paused at the top of the steps, my folder slick in my palm. My heart beat like I was about to jump from a plane. To my left was certainty, structure, family. To my right was the unknown.

Erica spotted me, and I walked to her. I hugged her, holding on tight.

"So you're not coming," she whispered. "I didn't think you would. Still—I hoped."

I let her go and stepped back. "If I went, it would be the Program forever. And now I knew what that really meant."

"Because you saw something else," Erica said.

I nodded. Tears streamed as I hugged the ones I was closest to, exchanging last words that felt too small for what we'd shared. I would miss them more than I could say. But I couldn't go.

The folder caught quick—first the corner, then the whole edge curling black, paper bowing inward as if exhaling. Papers and photographs dissolved into smoke. I watched them crumple into themselves, brittle as leaves, until they broke apart completely.

Heat licked my face, and for a moment it felt like the fire was breathing for me, taking in everything I'd carried and spitting it back out as ash. The smoke twisted upward, caught by the sunlight, drifting into the air like a trail of ghosts flickering out of existence.

This was who I had been. Evaluations. Test scores. Every way the Program thought it could define me. Gone. And still—I was here.

The Program had taught me how to endure, to keep going in the face of fear and exhaustion. It had taught me how to survive.

Now I have to teach myself how to live.

THE END